Underneath: Short Tales of Horror and the Supernatural

By Dan DeWitt

Copyright 2011 Dan DeWitt

TABLE OF CONTENTS

3 - Introduction
5 - Hope
12 - Dead After Dying
19 - Marriage Counseling
26 - One Simple Wish
39 - Father/Daughter Dance
48 - Sick Day
63 - Tigers
75 - Cupcakes
84 - Terror by Text
95 - How Many Years of Bad Luck
        Am I Up To, Anyway?
109 - Orpheus (Preview)

Introduction

The contemporary definition of the short story is a work of prose fiction 20,000 words or less.

20,000 words. That's approximately *eighty* pages.

I suppose that, technically, that would be a short story, but it's not exactly coffee break material.

I love to read, but I've always hated getting started on a short story that turns out to be novella length. One of my favorite authors pulled that on me in a short story collection: the first half was a bunch of great short stories, the second half a pretty uninteresting novella that I still have never gotten through. For people who like to read on their work breaks, for example, it can be frustrating to have to spread a short story over several 15-minute chunks. Granted, that's kind of a First World problem, but still.

I wrote the stories in "Underneath" with that in mind.

The longest of the tales in this book weighs in at a shade under 4,000 words (approximately sixteen pages). The shortest, just under 1,500 (six).

Unless, of course, you count the approximately 17,000 words' worth of *Orpheus* preview, but I don't think you'll mind. I made it a point to give you a large sample of the players, the situation, and the action before cutting it off at a natural stopping point.

Lastly, for you other aspiring writers out there, I slipped a contest into the last story. Read its brief afterword for details.

All of that being said, let me show you what's

underneath.

Dan DeWitt
20June2011

Hope

This is the only story that I have no idea where it came from. For every other story in this collection I can pinpoint a conversation, or an image, or something that made it want to be written. Not this one. I sat down to write some more of a novel-in-progress, but this is what came out. I really hope this guy finds what he's looking for.

* * *

He saw a silhouette a hundred feet away. The moon shone brightly enough for him to navigate along the quiet country road, but it was behind the sign and didn't illuminate the writing. He reached into the pouch at his hip and pulled out the flashlight without breaking stride. He put the beam on the sign as he walked and the reflective metal surface revealed, "Welcome to Haber! You'll Never Want to Leave!" *Haber*, he thought. *That's one of those Scandinavian languages. It's ringing a bell, for some reason.*

He checked his watch. The hands on the numberless face told him that it was 9:42. Sometimes, he felt like the last guy in the world who wore an honest-to-goodness traditional wristwatch. Growing up, it seemed that everyone, men and women, wore one everyday. Then came the Godawful digital ones, and then cell phones after that. But he'd held out. It never needed batteries or recharging, it kept perfect time, told him the date, he could even tell the direction by it if the

5

sun was out (a trick that he'd learned from a long-lost friend). The only thing it really lacked was a month indicator, and he had overcome that with a simple piece of tape. Twelve months, twelve hashes on the watch face...it was a low-tech solution, but it worked like a charm.

The date readout said "31." The tape was on the twelve o'clock hash. December. He hadn't realized it because his travel days really left him unconcerned with nothing but eating, sleeping, and putting one foot in front of the other, but it was New Year's Eve! That was a time for forgetting the past and remaking your future! He smiled. He hadn't done that in days; he'd been so disappointed by striking out in the previous town that he'd just set his feet to the pavement and started moving. Now, something as simple as a cheerful greeting and slogan had brought him back to where he always wanted to be. He believed the sign with all his heart.

His pace quickened until the road dropped away in a steep incline beneath his feet. Haber proper, it seemed, lay nestled in a valley, bathed in the soft glow of the moon, which only added to the air of small-town perfection that he felt. Granted, he'd felt that in the previous town, and the town before that, but this time was different. This time, Haber would be the town where he would find the one person who would make his journey of the last few years, the miles on his feet, the dozens of pairs of shoes, the lonely days and nights, worth it. The one person who would make him whole again.

He checked his watch again: 9:56. He'd been so enamored with Haber that fourteen minutes had passed

6

unnoticed. That was another good sign.

That person was down there somewhere, he knew it.

He knew it.

He didn't want to ruin everything by crashing the party early. He wanted to let Haber enjoy ringing out the old before inviting himself into their beautiful little community. A quick look around him revealed a row of wrought iron park benches looking over the town. More luck: this was an observation point, a place to get away from it all for a moment and just immerse yourself in what he assumed were magnificent sunsets over the town.

He moved to the closest one and removed his pack from his back. He'd barely bent over at the waist to sit when he heard a loud noise behind him and felt pressure on his hip. He yelped and jumped forward, then realized what it had been, and laughed at himself. It had been so long since he'd used it that he'd forgotten all about the rifle. He unslung it and leaned it up against the bench. The sidearm, he knew from experience, wouldn't get in the way, so he sat down and stretched out. He reached into his bag and grabbed a candy bar without looking. It was a Milky Way. There were a lot of Milky Ways in there. He occasionally washed it down with a sip of water from his insulated bottle. The crisp winter weather kept it refreshingly cold. He'd find a coffee down there later on, though. A good cup o' Joe was hard to find on the rarely-traveled country roads that he preferred to travel on. The highways just seemed so...impersonal...to him.

At this distance, the town was silent, but the silence wasn't absolute. The forest around him was alive with the sounds of its inhabitants going about business as usual, unconcerned with his presence. In his previous life, these kinds of moments, the moments where he blended in and nature forgot all about him, were rare. Now, since his rebirth as a wanderer who only tried to leave it as he had found it, they were par for the course, though no less peaceful or welcome. Their mating calls and fluttering wings drowned out any stray sounds that may have been coming from the town. Their celebrations must be muted here; it struck him as a reserved family town, and he envisioned a lot of small home celebrations as opposed to large bashes. He certainly could appreciate that.

He finished his candy bar, capped his water, and felt his eyelids getting heavy. He figured he could afford a nap. He put his pack on the bench and lay his head on it. He pulled the rifle across his chest and was asleep in minutes.

He awoke to the howling of a coyote. According to his watch, which had never failed him, he'd been asleep for just over four hours.

It was time to meet Haber.

His laces felt loose, so he bent over to retie them. As he did, an object on a chain fell loose through his open collar. He absentmindedly held the diamond ring in his hand, confused.

Where did I...?

Then he remembered. He'd known a guy once, a good friend of his, Dave, whose wife had died suddenly. In fact, she'd gone from sick to dead in a few short hours, and she had been in agony until the last. By the time Dave was determined to end her suffering for her, she was dead on the couch. In her death spasms, she had thrown her left arm out, where it came to its final resting place on the coffee table, right next to the open bottle of champagne and two crystal glasses. They'd been celebrating something, though he couldn't remember what.

He'd offered his condolences, but her death had broken Dave. He kept talking about going to find his wife, in complete denial that she was gone. He'd tried to reason with him, but Dave, determined to "find" her, had simply...gone. He really couldn't blame him; though he himself had never been married, he understood that the two of them had been deeply in love and he wasn't surprised at his friend's reaction. He wasn't sure that he wouldn't have done the same thing in his place.

Left alone with her body, he didn't know what to do. He wanted to give her a proper burial, but the December ground had been far too hard. So he'd carried her upstairs to the bedroom she and her husband had shared, arranged her in a peaceful pose, and said the best prayer he could think of.

He began to pull a sheet over her, but his eyes were drawn to her ring finger and the beautiful diamond on her hand. Fearful that someone would steal it, he slid it gently off of her hand and attached it to a simple chain he found in her dresser. He slipped it around his neck, kissed her forehead, and covered her. If he ever found Dave, he'd gladly return the ring, but it didn't feel right to just leave such a special thing unprotected.

Hope. Her name had been Hope. That's why the town sounded familiar; "Haber" was Danish for "Hope."

Why do I know that?

After taking a moment to appreciate the coincidence, he finished tying his boots, put the rest of his gear back on, and began walking toward the town.

When he got closer to town, he took off his pack again and stuck his hand in. He'd proven to himself a long time ago that the sickness did not and probably would not ever affect him, but the smell in these towns was often overpowering, even in the cold weather.

He rummaged through his pack for the mask. He pulled it out along with a Ziploc bag that had been with him since the beginning of his journey. He flipped through the contents. The tourist pamphlets showcased names like Hope Ridge, New Hope, Hope Falls, and Espoir, among others. Memories flooded his mind, all of them pretty much the same. Each place had a promising start but, eventually, he'd left each one without finding that person.

Those had all been merely way stations, though. Just places to rest and restock. Haber had always been his true destination. He knew that now.

He put the pamphlets back in the bag. He would throw them out as soon as he met the person he was looking for. That minute. That second. Because once he was with that person, he wouldn't need the memories of failure to drive him anymore. He would have found that love that had eluded him for his entire life. A love like Dave once had.

He tried to adjust the straps of the mask for a snug fit, but his fingers were clumsy inside of the thick gloves. He pulled them off and had much more success. He took a few test breaths, was satisfied, and started to put his left glove on, but was stopped by a glint of metal on his hand.

A wedding ring.
Where did I...?

Then he remembered. He'd known a guy once, a good friend of his...

Dead After Dying

This is the first of three zombie tales in the book. I love zombies; that's really all you need to know.

* * *

People who watched Donnie and me together as little kids often commented to my parents that we were closer than brothers. When I got old enough to hear those stories related to me, I understood that they were right. I have...had...a relative who fit the biological definition of a brother, but Donnie and I were much closer than that. We had a motto between us. More like a vow, really. I know that's something that kids just do, and then forget about as life takes hold, but we meant it.

"Beyond the end." We'd always be there for each other, no matter what. The end of school, a relationship, even death itself, we truly believed with the innocence of children...none of those things would keep us apart.

And we held to that vow. Even as those walking nightmares turned our town into a slaughterhouse and ate (or worse, turned) everyone we loved, we held to that vow. I was there with Donnie, holding his hand, telling him that we wouldn't be apart long, as the blood, too much blood, pooled beneath both of us on the frigid tile floor of the restaurant kitchen. I was there to help him along to the next step, whatever that might be, and I closed his pale blue eyes after he was gone.

And I was there when those eyes popped back open and he lunged for my throat. To my credit, I didn't run right away. I tried to help him. Then I tried to kill him, because I knew that he wouldn't want to be like that. I just didn't have anything to kill him with, and he wasn't giving me the time to look.

So I ran, coatless but fortunately wearing good boots, into the freak October blizzard, with Donnie on my heels.

There was almost no hope. I knew it then, I know it now. But instinct compelled me to try. No weapon to kill him with meant none for me, either. The best-case scenario was that I would freeze to death before Donnie could get to me.

I could live with that. That thought was okay with me. Even though Donnie was gone...far, far gone...I just couldn't let the thing that wore his face feast on his best friend. That's an insult that I refused to allow.

The first few minutes weren't too bad. I moved through the snow pretty well, putting some distance between me and him. Mind you, I was still aware that, though I was running from him, I was also running towards the same abominations that had taken the neighboring town. Again, it didn't matter. As the saying goes, I was headed nowhere, but making great time.

Then the cold hit me.

Hard.

And, because God or Mother Nature or whatever thinks he/she/it is hilarious, the snow intensified to the point where I could only see a few inches in front of my face. The wind whipped up, too, but that, at least, was at my back.

I could feel a gentle numbing in my ears first. I rubbed them as I powered through the increasing snow cover, but that only served to numb my fingers even faster. The numbness traveled inward, taking my forearms, upper arms, shoulders, neck.

But my feet? Good as ever.

Excellent boots.

I looked behind me. I couldn't be sure, but it looked like Donnie was gaining little by little. Even if he wasn't, even if my slowly-freezing head was playing tricks on me, it was only a matter of time. I didn't have to be a scientist to figure out that he didn't feel, couldn't feel, what I felt. He had a good half-inch of snow on him, whereas I only had a dusting. My otherwise-unoccupied mind theorized that was because, frankly, he was dead, and gave off no body heat to melt the snow from him. I imagined that the coating would be the only way that an observer would be able to tell which one of us was living and which was not.

The end was getting close. I didn't even try to deny it; I long-jumped over the first four stages of grief and landed right on acceptance. The best plan I could come up with was to get someplace inaccessible to Donnie so I could save both whatever was left of his soul and myself some serious hurt. Maybe, if I was lucky enough and there were survivors somewhere (please, God, let there be survivors), I would present something suitable for burial.

Even near death, it was important to have a goal in mind. Otherwise, what was the damn point? Of anything?

I willed myself to look around at my surroundings, at the woods I grew up playing in. Hide and seek gave way to pseudo-camping to paintball to our unsuccessful attempt to start smoking to making out with Gwennie Barber in...

...in the cave.

I was close.

It wasn't the cave proper that I was actually interested in, but rather the steep incline in front of it. I just didn't think that Donnie, whose coordination was shot to shit, could handle it. I wasn't entirely positive I could, either, but it was my best bet.

I looked back again. Now there was no doubt. He'd closed the gap. I hooked as sharp a left as I could manage and concentrated on my march: lift left foot, push, stomp. Lift right foot, push, stomp. Repeat.

I was there.

The incline looked intimidating to me. In my youth, after Donnie and I had figured out the path of least resistance, we'd take whatever girl we'd been dating at the time here. Or try to, anyway. The seclusion was a big part of the attraction, of course, but so was the climb. Any girl who'd be willing to climb it with us, well...there would be no mistaking their willingness. Neither Donnie nor I ever failed to, at bare minimum, get boob. Twice, I actually scored. Regardless of outcome, as I got a little older I realized that it was nice just knowing that they'd all trusted me enough to lead them, hand-in-hand, up a hill into a dark cave in the middle of nowhere.

Gwennie had been the last girl to make that climb with me. Then I got a car, and the world opened itself to me and my libido. For all I knew, the candles that we burned that night were still there. I had no matches, but it was comforting, to a degree.

I wanted Gwennie to be okay. I knew she almost certainly wasn't. Still, I hoped.

You probably don't care about any of this.

15

I reached the bottom and grabbed onto the first branch. This same branch had been the only starting point for every successful climb. Start anywhere else, and you'd end up at the bottom again (and not necessarily by choice). Donnie learned that the hard way, and still had the scar on his knee to prove it. I just about died laughing that day.

I couldn't feel the branch. I...I looked at my hand and saw that I hadn't even grasped it. It was just sort of resting there, Donnie's blood sticking out as the only colorful thing against a whitewashed background. I willed my hand to close, but no movement.

So that was it.

I turned around. Donnie was just too close now.

I collapsed onto my ass in the snow and rested my back against the tree.

All I wanted now was to hold him off long enough to die. Then, Donnie could do...what those things do best.

I heard the sound of snow crunching underfoot. I turned my head as quickly as I could (not quickly at all), and saw another human shape. I had a momentary burst of hope that I'd been rescued, but the frozen blood that had turned a white button-down shirt almost entirely crimson dashed those thoroughly. Maybe someone else had found themselves in a similar situation as mine. I'd fared a little better, for whatever that was worth.

It made a snarling noise and moved for me.

Donnie was on it immediately.

I'd seen this kind of behavior before. These things wouldn't eat each other that I knew of. They were, however, territorial as all Hell. At that moment, I was the territory, and I did something that I'd never done before in my entire life: I rooted against my best friend. I wanted the other thing to put Donnie down for good and, if it had to come to that, be the one that finished me off. Two birds, one undead stone.

Donnie, curse him, showed the same indefatigable resolve that I'd seen so often on the basketball court. He tore that thing apart. Quite literally. A severed arm landed close enough to me that I could have reached out and touched it. Or it, me.

He turned to me, all business again.

I tried to raise my arms in front of me, protect my face, my neck, anything. Nothing was working right.

Except for my feet. Still toasty warm.

I tried to focus on that feeling as Donnie dropped to his knees three feet in front of me and leaned in, teeth bared. He moved slowly. Even though he couldn't feel the cold, it was still doing a number on his body. Unless the weather broke soon, he'd eventually freeze, too, right next to whatever remained of yours truly.

I summoned every last bit of me to whisper something. I don't know how successfully my lifeless lips relayed the message, but what I was going for was, "Beyond the end, buddy." My eyelids drooped, and I began to slip away.

Donnie stopped.

Stared.

He was close enough that I could smell him. There was no smell of decay; he hadn't been dead that long. He smelled like cheap light beer.

He twitched, then sat back on his heels.

Stared.

I already know what you're going to think. That

the cold had finally broken him down, as it had me. Or maybe he smelled the death on me and decided that I would be unpalatable. Or a host of other reasons. All or none of the things that pass through your head may have been true. But whatever else you may think, I don't really care.

I know...*I know*...what I saw in his eyes. A spark of recognition. Momentary. Instantaneous. Unrecognizable to anyone who wasn't at the edge of oblivion.

Real.

My mouth curved into what I think was a smile.

We win, Donnie. One last time, we win.

Feeling strangely protected, I closed my eyes, embraced the end, and went to see what waited beyond.

Marriage Counseling

File this under the classic theme of, "Be careful what you wish for."

* * *

"If you need confirmation that your wife is cheating on you, I can give it."

A few months ago, Ray Dropp would have been surprised, or even angered, by the words of the man sitting in the passenger seat of his SUV. "Yeah, I figured. Bitch."

"I'd be remiss if I didn't give you an opportunity to call it off. It would be as if we never met, minus the deposit, of course."

Dropp looked at the man he had come to think of as his an independent contractor, his personal Mr. Fix-it, and shook his head. "No way." Mr. Fix-it accepted the answer wordlessly, but Dropp continued on. "You know, we actually tried marriage counseling once. I remember the counselor, this real homo, kept on about how we should do these communication exercises. It was the biggest waste of time, because that wasn't the problem. The problem's that she's a little whore. It's not just that, either. The punchline is that she's not getting my money."

"Hmmm," was the reply.

"What's that?"

Mr. Fix-it looked straight ahead, through the rain-soaked windshield. "I've heard the same story more times than I can count. It's pretty common in my line of work. A few haven't gone through with it; most have. I often wonder how many people regret their decision either way." He shifted gears. "What I do is permanent. Just so you understand this."

"Yeah, I get it, I get it. When?" Dropp listened to the details. He couldn't wait for tomorrow night.

* * *

Dropp followed the tail lights of his wife's Toyota. She thought he was out of town on business, so between that and the rain he wasn't concerned about her spotting him. He knew that Mr. Fix-it was in the passenger seat, because they were heading to a motel just outside of town. He had apparently planted the seeds for an affair during the week or so he had spent

19

gathering information. He really was very good. A week! It had taken Dropp three to get into her pants when they had first started dating. She'd apparently conquered her intimacy issues since then.

Dropp cared about none of this. He just wanted to watch her die, and he had been very specific about this. He had no doubt that Mr. Fix-it would deliver. Hell, he might have some fun with Melanie first, and more power to him. She was a lot of things, but a lousy lay certainly wasn't one of them. Maybe he'd even drop the price a little.

They arrived at the motel. Mr. Fix-it had rented two rooms in advance, so there would be no messing with the desk clerk. No witnesses, either. Mr. Fix-it and Melanie got out of the car, and she was hanging all over him on the way to number 32. They entered the room, shut the door, and pulled the shades.

Now, the wait.

"Thirty minutes," Mr. Fix-it had said. "On the nose."

Dropp was anxious, but he wouldn't be the one to screw this up. He set the alarm on his watch for twenty-nine minutes and nodded off.

* * *

The beeping watch snapped Dropp awake. He rubbed the sleep out of his eyes, snatched the key to number 33 off of the seat, and entered the room as quietly as possible. He left the door slightly ajar, as instructed. He sat on the edge of the bed, grabbed the remote that he was told would be there, and turned to the auxiliary channel. Instead of snow or just a black

20

screen, he had a great color view of the king-size bed in Room 32, as well as its occupants, who were sitting and embracing on the bed. Mr. Fix-it's back was to the camera, but there was no mistaking Melanie. The two broke the kiss, and Dropp got his first good look at his dear wife. Her hair looked fantastic, and she had even broken out some gorgeous lingerie that he had never seen before. "Unbelievable," he muttered.

On-screen, Mr. Fix-it spoke to her, and she mouthed something in return and reached for her purse. She rummaged through it casually at first, then with a bit more urgency. She upended it, but couldn't find what she had been looking for. Dropp was no lip-reader, but he could make out, "I'm sorry," coming from her pouty, crimson lips. Her would-be lover said something and poured her a short glass of wine, which she downed in a few swallows. He poured her another, kissed her on the neck, and left the room. Dropp went to his window and saw Mr. Fix-it get into her car and drive away.

"Now where the Hell is he going?" Dropp wondered aloud. Wherever it was, he had not been made privy to it, but he was sure it was part of the plan.

He forget entirely about Mr. Fix-it (and indeed, why he was here at all) when Melanie began slowly exploring her body in anticipation of her lover's return. Dropp was mesmerized, and almost missed the fact that she was staring at the camera. Not only was she aware of it, but she was performing for it.

That kinky bitch, Dropp thought, and for a split-second wondered if he was making a mistake. His rational mind took over and educated him that she had never performed for him that way. This realization only strengthened his resolve. Still, he enjoyed the show, and wondered how long he had before Mr. Fix-it returned.

It wasn't long, and he jumped when the man walked through the door.

"Where have you been?" Dropp asked, his question unintentionally laced with accusation. He regretted it when Mr. Fix-it shot him a subtle look that made him shut up immediately.

"Condoms. I told her I forgot them, and I had to run out to get some."

"She's been cheating on me for God knows how long, and she didn't bring condoms? Jesus, she could be carrying anything! *I* could be carrying anything!"

"Relax. She had some, but I took them out of her purse. I drove around the corner and came back here. Are you ready?"

"You bet your ass. When's it happening?"

"It's happening now. Do you see that wine on the table?"

"Yup."

"Poison. She'll be dead in ten minutes. She's dying, and you're watching, as we agreed."

It was done. There was no turning back now, so Dropp wanted to enjoy this.

"Now for the matter of payment."

Dropp was emboldened by the power he felt. "You'll get it as soon as she's dead."

"Not what we agreed on, but fair enough. I can wait."

"Shit, I feel like celebrating. I need a cigar or something."

Mr. Fix-it reached into the pocket of his leather coat. He pulled out three cigars of various brands. "On the house."

Dropp examined the selection. "Nice. My favorites." He considered them for another moment and selected one.

"I do my homework, Raymond." He took the cigar from him, cut it expertly, and then lit it as Dropp held it to his lips.

Dropp, a former two-pack-a-day cigarette smoker, inhaled deeply. Most cigar smokers didn't inhale. Those people, Dropp thought, were wimps. He watched the screen, and Melanie made a small jerking movement, followed by another, larger one.

"Her lungs are beginning to shut down, so screaming is out of the question. She'll suffer for a few minutes, but she'll be aware enough to see this." He pulled a remote control out of his pocket, and clicked a button. On the screen, Melanie's eyes grew wide in surprise. She was looking in the direction of her own television. In Room 33, Dropp noticed a red light come on inside of the air conditioning vent.

"What's that?"

"A camera. She can see us. A smart woman like that will have figured it out by now."

Dropp took another puff. "Nice touch."

"I know."

Dropp was so transfixed by the look of terror in his wife's eyes that he almost didn't feel the itching in his throat. It was regret, or guilt, he supposed.

"You know, you really should have taken your counseling more seriously."

Dropp found himself slightly short of breath, but forced out, "Wh-why's that?"

"Because the two of you have a lot more in common than you think."

The cigar fell from Dropp's fingers as he fell backwards on the bed, clutching his throat. Mr. Fix-it hovered over him and slipped a hand inside of Dropp's pants pocket. *He knows where the money is. Of course he knows.* He thought he was screaming for help, but no sound would come out.

"Except she paid me in advance."

One Simple Wish

I love this story. I started it with the intention of it becoming a novel, but I knew right away that it had no chance of being that long. I merely stripped out a few catalytic elements and it shortened itself. I submitted it to various places, and it was well-received, but no one thought it fit their genre. They were right, of course, but I still think it deserves a spot in the book.

* * *

On a snowy night that might have been Christmas Eve, a desperate man (his name is irrelevant, though John will do) resigned himself to killing his wife. As he walked slowly down the hall, knowing that he would soon end his own life, as well, the little girl in the room just before his destination called him "Daddy."

He stopped just outside her door and sight. He tried to ignore her and listen harder at the same time, but he failed at both. She repeated, "Daddy?"

Just keep walking, he told himself. You'll only make it harder. It's always difficult to argue with your inner voice, your conscience, especially when you are in absolute agreement with it. He had a job to do, and the sooner, the better. Still, he hesitated, and it was the next sentence that hooked him.

"Daddy, where's Troy? I think he ran outside." Her voice cracked, just a little. He cracked much harder, and for no good reason (or every good reason) he walked in the room, sat down on the bed next to her and said, "Daddy's here, baby." She smiled without opening her eyes, and she felt around for his hand. He helped her find it. Her hand was so fragile in the embrace of his, like an innocent little girl's should be.

"Go to sleep, sweetie."

"But I can't go to sleep without Troy!"

He fumbled for a response, and came up with, "I think he's downstairs eating."

"He already ate." Her voice cracked a little more, and grew a little smaller. "He already ate."

He looked out the window. The snowfall was impressive, to say the least. No way was he going to look for a dog in that mess. No way at all.

He caught himself by surprise when he said, "I'll take a look outside. I promise."

What am I doing?

Her eyes snapped open. Of course they were that beautiful shade of blue. "Thank you, Daddy!"

He choked out, "Now try to sleep, sweetie."

He got up. He supposed he should have wondered why he was suddenly feeling dizzy, but he didn't have to. He took two steps toward the door, turned around, bent over and kissed her on the forehead. He expected her to feel warm to his lips, but she was slightly cool. "I'll be back in a little bit." He pulled the blanket up to her neck, grabbed a photo of Troy to show to people, and walked out without looking back.

Once he was back in the hallway, he looked left to where he had been heading in the first place. She would be sleeping; he could almost hear her slowed heartbeat, and how it would pump like a jackhammer as she fought for breath for the few moments it would take for her to give up. It would be so easy. He knew that a decision had to be made, and he also knew that it had been decided as soon as soon as "Daddy?" had reached his ears. He knew that girl's future, and he was not going to make one of his last acts on this Earth deceiving one who trusted him so completely, if naively.

So he turned right, walked down the stairs, each footfall making a dull thud…like a slowed heartbeat.

John reached the bottom of the stairs, paused, and sighed. He pushed the door open, turned up his collar, and let the storm envelop him.

* * *

His truck was parked only a few feet away, still running. He had planned on killing his wife and leaving quickly. In the dead of night, in this storm, he didn't worry about anyone seeing him. Even if he was unfortunate enough to have someone see him driving away, there was no way they could identify him or know where he was going. He would just be a nut with four-wheel drive, out on a night when no one should be. If everything went according to plan, he and his truck would never be found at the bottom of the lake, because he didn't deserve to be found.

He had a little time to look for the kid's dog, though. That way he could at least tell the truth when he told her he couldn't find Troy. She would probably cry, but that wouldn't last too long. He'd be gone by then. He decided he'd walk around calling for the dog for a half hour or so; he could use the fresh air. He grabbed the car keys, and the plastic bag holding the cigar he planned on smoking at the lake just before…just before. *What the hell*, he thought, *now or later, makes no difference, but I* am *smoking this tonight.*

27

After about ten minutes of walking, John found himself downtown. The main drag really was beautiful under the blanket of the snowstorm, and it didn't hurt that there were no humans anywhere to screw it up. He breathed deep, savoring the crisp air, when a blast of icy wind and snow hit him square in the face. He turned away from it as fast as he could, which wasn't quite fast enough. He felt like he had been slapped with an open hand, and it brought a tear to his eye.

As he blinked it away, he saw the dog. Barely, but he saw the damn thing, standing under the eaves of Darby's Barber Shop (Darby's sign in the window, "$8 Trim", was always a chuckle-inducer for the men in town who had a sophomoric sense of humor, which was, naturally, all of the men in town). Reflexively he reached into his coat pocket and pulled out the dog's picture, but of course he didn't have to. He tried to sound friendly, in spite of the storm, as he yelled, "Troy! Here boy!" The dog perked at his name. He cocked his head at the man walking slowly toward him, and it seemed he was waiting to be picked up.

The dog waited until the man was about five feet away before he bolted and disappeared around a corner.

Damn. A chase it is, then.

He broke into a jog. John ran several miles a week, so the bulky coat didn't present much of a problem. The footing wasn't all that bad, and he could see the tracks in the snow, so perseverance, and not speed, would be the key. He figured that the dog's tiny little legs would only carry him so far before he got tired, bored, or distracted by an attractive hydrant. He rounded the corner and loped down the alley, or, rather, an impression of an alley. It was merely the space between a restaurant and a computer repair shop. Clean and well-lit, it was nothing like the corridors of darkness seen in the movies, the kind of places where you just knew something bad was waiting for either star or bit player. As he walked, he passed a few garbage cans. With little thought, he opened one of them and rooted through it, looking for something that a dog might find appetizing. He found it beneath a ripped bra and an empty box of Triscuits: a chicken bone, some meat still hanging on it. He grabbed it by the cleanest, driest part and tried not to think how gross the whole experience was.

He was right about the dog; he hadn't gotten far before stopping to urinate on a nearby snow-covered bush. John whistled for him and waved the chicken bone. The dog showed some interest, but turned and walked into a large clearing.

The snow blew harder, threatening to take the dog from his sight. John quickened his pace, trying to walk sideways to avoid facing directly into the storm. He caught a glimpse of Troy, lost him, then found him again when he barked. The dog was actually playing a game with him.

Troy stood motionless in the center of the clearing. John heaved the bone in his direction, and it buried itself in the snow. The dog leaped to the spot and buried its snout in the thickening snow cover, tearing at the bone. John moved towards him. The dog noticed this, but gave him a look that said he would accept some company now, that the bribe had worked. Confident that his impromptu quest was nearing its end, he reached the dog and began to bend down to him.

It was then that he heard the first crack, followed

closely by a second.

Ice.

The dog led him into the center of not a clearing, but a pond.

John knew with the third crack that there was nowhere for him to go but down. The too-thin crust of the pond broke, and John's large frame plunged straight down into water so cold that it felt hot. It hit him all at once, and his body began to shut down almost immediately as his head dropped below the surface. He shot a hand up, blindly groping for purchase on the side of the hole, but he could find nothing but a solid sheet. Somehow, in the span of just a few seconds, he had drifted away from the considerable hole in the ice. It occurred to him then that this was similar to how he had already planned to end his night, though he had skipped the part about killing his wife and went straight to drowning, instead.

His hand found something. It was not the ragged edge of a freshly-made hole, no. It felt more like a dog's leather collar. He tried to look up, but his body didn't respond. He merely held to the collar, feeling that the dog was tugging backwards. It wasn't the frantic movement of a dog trying to escape. It felt more like the animal was actually trying to pull him out, losing proposition or not. With fading lucidity, John understood that there was no possible outcome other than dragging this dog down with him, and there was just no sense in that. With great effort, he released the collar. He drifted down, down, and the darkness crept in around the edges until it overtook him.

John never felt the hand reach down and pull him out.

* * *

When he woke, he was lying on top of the ice, shivering. He was alone; very alone. The storm had waned, the moon shone brightly, and he could see for hundreds of yards in every direction. Whoever had saved him was long gone. They had given him a second chance at life, and didn't stick around long enough to find out how he intended to waste it. He struggled to his feet, amazed that he could move at all. He had no idea how long he had been lying in the snow, but it had been long enough for the storm to cover the approaching and retreating footsteps of his unidentified rescuer.

But he had only a faint dusting of snow on him, so he couldn't have been lying unexposed for long.

He was convinced that he had never fallen through the ice. That had to have been some kind of delusion, because he wasn't wet.

A few seconds later, he realized that wasn't entirely true: one sleeve was in danger of freezing solid, as it had been dipped in water up to the shoulder.

What the hell just happened? John wondered, trying to get his bearings both physical and mental.

He began to trudge carefully back the way he had first come, sure that direction would be safe, as he had already traversed it once. He jammed his hands deep into his pockets, and his numb fingers closed upon an object that could only be a waterlogged dog collar.

* * *

John stared through the window of the toy shop,

31

despondent because he had failed to catch a dog for a worried little girl. He couldn't even grant that one simple wish. He had learned long ago (more than three years ago, in fact) that wishes were never horses. It was shame that she would know it at such a young age, too. He sighed and began to travel back to where, he hoped, she would be sleeping peacefully, and threw a casual glance back at the toy store for no reason at all. In that moment he saw an object that had escaped his notice for the ten minutes or so he had stared directly at it. It was a stuffed dog, and it looked disturbingly like good ol' Troy.

That's too weird, John thought. *That can't be coincidence.*

He decided that he needed that dog, and he wasn't above breaking and entering to get it. He had enough cash on him to cover the cost of the toy and the lock, as well. It won't do me any good where I'm going, anyway. He grasped the knob, looked furtively around him, knowing that the chances anyone else was foolish enough to be out this late on a night like this were remote, and opened the unlocked door with little problem. Only the tinkle of the bell above the door broke the silence.

Definitely not a coincidence.

He moved quickly, grabbed the dog, checked the price tag and did a double take. "That much? I'd have a hard time paying that for a real dog," he said to the empty room. "Empty" only applied to other people; a hundred sets of eyes still stared at him. John noticed their plastic gaze. What otherwise would have been creepy seemed almost…approving. He opened his wallet, emptied it, and left more than enough cash neatly arranged on the counter next to the register.

He closed the door firmly behind him, double-checking to ensure it was locked.

* * *

John paused in the doorway, clutching the toy dog. It had seemed right to put Troy's (wherever he was) collar around the doll's neck, so he had.

"Daddy?" That same fragile voice asked.

"I'm here, sweetie." He sat on the bed next to her.

"Did you find him?"

He gritted his teeth. *She's out of it; she won't notice. I hope.* "Yeah. He's okay. Why don't you go to sleep now?"

She was drifting down again. She yawned, "I love you, Daddy,"

He kissed her on her forehead, told her he loved her, too, and tucked the toy dog into the crook of her arm (*Please don't let her notice*). She went to sleep with a smile, warm and content. He watched her for a few minutes, and shed some tears for her. He was not ashamed.

John collected himself and walked to the door. He looked at her one last time. She was beautiful, and he would hold that picture in his mind until the end.

He went to talk to the night nurse.

* * *

"Excuse me, but the little girl in there."

The nurse helped him out. "Carolyn."

"Carolyn. Why is she here?" He was afraid of the answer.

That answer came in the form of a disease that John could barely pronounce. "She doesn't have long. But she's been an angel the whole time she's been here."

He swallowed hard. "Where are her parents?"

A shake of the nurse's head told him all he needed to know. She sprung from her chair as an alarm went off. John knew without looking that the alarm came from little Carolyn's room, and he was certain what it meant. He watched the nurse leave to do her job and discover what he already knew. He left the desk area and entered the room two doors down from Carolyn's. This was his best chance, now while the nurse was distracted.

His wife, Denise, lay there, as she had for just over three years, ever since a night a lot like this one conspired to take her from him. It had succeeded in destroying them both. She was comatose, with little chance for recovery. He was healthy, and had no chance. Many nights he had come close to doing what had to be done and had chickened out, if that was an appropriate term for deciding against murder. Tonight, however, he was determined.

She. Wouldn't. Want. This.

He reached for a pillow, and saw the toy dog, nestled in the crook of her arm. He staggered backwards several steps. There was no mistaking that it was the same doll; it wore a collar that still looked a little wet. He moved forward again, confused. He poked the dog as if it were an illusion. His wife moaned a little bit, but she had done that many times before; the doctors had repeatedly told him it was an involuntary reaction, and his optimism had faded a little more each time until he had none left.

She moaned a second time, and, just as he knew that Carolyn had gone without seeing her, he knew that this noise wasn't like all the rest. He stared at her; he was sure he saw her eyes move behind the lids, like she was merely dreaming. Maybe it was just wishful thinking, but it was enough. He leaned into her ear and said, "I'm sorry, baby. I stopped believing in you for a while. I was wrong. Don't make me wait long, okay?" He kissed her on each cheek, tucked the dog in a little more snugly, and walked down the hall. He glanced into Carolyn's room and saw the nurse standing over her, possibly reciting a prayer for the poor girl. What he didn't see was a toy dog.

The snow still fell, but the wind gusts had turned into soft breaths, and he reached into his pocket. He pulled out the cigar which, another miracle, was intact and bone dry. He clipped it, flipped open the butane torch, and lit it slowly and deliberately, careful to not miss a spot. He took a deep draw and held it; it was better than he could have hoped. He sat on the cold steps and passed time by focusing on an individual flake as it fell to the ground, and then another after that.

The door opened behind him. It was the nurse. "Did you know her?" she asked him plainly, as she wrapped her coat around her.

He considered telling her the whole story, but decided against it. "No. She just looked lonely." He took another draw and blew it downwind from the nurse. "Is there anyone to take care of her?"

"The state."

"I don't think so. Send it all my way. Everything.

I don't care who I have to go through."

The nurse looked ready to respond when they both turned towards the sound of scratching at the door. "Hey!" the nurse exclaimed. "Is that your dog?" She opened the door and let Troy out. He bounded towards John and licked his hand.

What the hell, John thought. "Yeah. He is."

Father/Daughter Dance

Being a father of a young boy myself, writing anything involving children (of any age, really) affects me much more now. I also have a better grasp of how far I'd go to protect him. But this is just an innocent dance in a small town, right?

* * *

"You know something, sweetheart," Jarv Wheeler said to his daughter mid-waltz, "this is always my favorite night of the year."

Dahlia looked at him, amused confusion on her face. "Favorite night of the year, Dad? Unless you have a secret daughter, this is our first father/daughter dance." She giggled.

He stumbled briefly. "Well, you know what I mean. I've been looking forward to this for a long time, that's all. Now mind your feet; remember, it's a box."

"Sorry. I know. My feet feel a little weird."

Damn. "Do you want to sit down?"

"For just a minute, yeah."

They went back to their table. She watched the other dancers. He watched her closely.

"I thought that I'd know more people here. A lot of my friends said they'd be coming."

"Well, it's early, and this dance is way out of town. I'm sure that they're on the way. Me, I don't do 'fashionably late' anymore. Cuts into my pre-bedtime naptime."

"You're so old."

"No argument here. Are you thirsty? Diet Coke or something?"

"Sure."

Jarv rose and planted a kiss on her forehead. She smiled and turned her attention back to the dance floor as he headed to the bar. He put a foot up on the brass rail and signaled to the bartender, who came over almost immediately. "What'll it be, boss?"

"Gin and tonic and a Sprite, please."

"You got it." The bartender began to pour the gin and asked, "Which one's yours?"

"What? Oh," he gestured in Dahlia's direction. "Black dress, red sash."

"Beautiful girl," the bartender replied without a hint of lecherousness. "Got her mother's looks, I see."

Jarv laughed a genuine laugh. "I count that as a blessing every day, my friend." He took a sip of his drink, nodded, and dropped a five into the tip jar. "Every damn day." He air-toasted the bartender and walked back to the table. Dahlia was rubbing a hand on her calf, as if it had fallen asleep. He checked his watch, and his heart sank. He took a deep breath and plastered on a smile. He put the drinks down and said, "Here you go, sweetie. They were out of Diet Coke. Sprite okay?"

"Sure." She took a healthy sip and rubbed her leg some more.

"Does your leg hurt?"

"It doesn't hurt. It's just kind of...numb. Maybe my shoes are too tight."

"Maybe. You think another dance would wake them up?"

She kicked off her shoes and said, "Let's find out!"

The DJ put on a fast number, something with a heavy dance beat that Jarv had no hope of recognizing. He heard a few girlish squeals that signified that this was currently a big teen hit. Dahlia furrowed her brow and said, "I don't think I've heard this before." The expression on some other faces suggested they thought the same thing. She stopped caring in a hurry, threw her hands in the air, and did what happy teen girls do: tear up the dance floor. If her legs still bothered her, she either didn't notice or didn't care.

He did his best to keep up.

A few minutes later, the DJ mercifully segued into a slow number, and Jarv, breathing hard, enveloped his daughter in his arms. "How are you feeling?" he whispered.

"A little better, I think." She rested her head on his shoulder. "That's funny...I don't remember this song, either..."

He kissed the top of her head and thought, *Too soon.*

    *   *   *

When the dance was over, he lifted her head. Her eyelids fluttered but didn't fully open. He blinked away the beginnings of tears. *I'm getting the timing down, at least. That's something...no, that's nothing. Nothing at all.* He shook her a little, but got no response.

"Is everything okay, sir?"

Jarv turned around and saw one of the chaperones, a woman about his age who looked dishearteningly familiar. She wore a look that was half-concern, half-reproach. "Oh, yes, I just think that my daughter might have confused my drink for hers."

The woman smiled. "That does seem to happen at these things sometimes. We have a few cots available, if..."

"No, I think we're going to call it a night."

"Of course. Let me walk you to your car." She walked a few paces ahead of them and handled the doors.

Jarv had Dahlia's arm around his neck and wrestled her to his truck. He fumbled with his keys and dropped them. The woman (he still didn't know her name) picked them up and deftly unlocked the passenger door. He placed her in the seat and she handled the seatbelt. He closed the door gently. "Thank you."

"My pleasure, Mr..."

"Jarvis Wheeler."

"Jarvis. I'm Maggie Tynes. I'm what you might call a councilwoman here. One of our duties, the rest of the council and I, is to chaperone this gathering. I recognize you. You were here last year. Had a similar experience, as well, if I remember correctly. I always remember correctly."

He didn't respond.

She pulled a pen out of her breast pocket. "Give me your hand." He held it out to her, and she began to scribble on his palm. "As you've done this at least twice, I can assume that you've gleaned a lot of information, just not quite enough. You wouldn't be the first to falter like this. This," she released his hand back to him, "should solve your problem."

He stared at his palm. *My God. That's it.*

40

"I'm not going to ask how you found our dance. What I will implore you to do is be discreet about who you share your knowledge with."

He still said nothing, but nodded.

"Very discreet."

"I understand."

"But when you do decide to share, and you will, share it fully so that we can avoid a repeat of your...amateurish attempt. It's not fair to the young women, and I don't enjoy watching it happen time and again. Every time I interject myself into others' affairs I put my own position at risk."

Jarv fumbled for the proper thank you. He impulsively kissed her on the lips. She met him, shared the kiss, and it was over.

"It's been a long time since a man has done that. Longer than you can imagine. Now go. I hope to never see you again."

"I'll try."

* * *

Jarv put his hands under his daughter and lifted. Her weight was a welcome burden; he'd bear it forever, if he could.

She stirred and her eyes opened. "Daddy?"

"Yes, baby?"

"Are we home?"

"Not yet. almost."

"Oh. Okay. I'm just really tired."

"Then sleep, sweetheart. I'll take care of everything."

"Can we have one more dance? I think I can

dance one more."

A "no" formed on Jarv's lips, but he bit it back. Selfishly, he supposed. "If you think you're up to it." He maneuvered her feet to the ground and tested to see if she could bear her weight.

"I totally am." To prove her point, she released her arms from around his neck and stood, unsteadily, but on her own.

Jarv reached through the car window and turned the radio up. He held her right hand with his left and placed his right gently on her waist, ready to catch her on a moment's notice.

She made it through the entire dance, but had closed her eyes somewhere along the way. "Thank you for the dance, Daddy. I think I need to shut my eyes for a little while." Her last words faded away, but Jarv could make out, "...don't know that song, either..."

He hugged her fiercely and whispered into her ear, "That's because it came out after you died."

He held her upright with one arm and popped his trunk. He pulled out a flashlight, cradled her once more, and walked into the woods, following the path that he'd first taken a year to the day after she'd been ripped away from him. Murdered by four otherwise unconnected animals with nothing better to do than take what they wanted from a pretty girl whose only sin was sneaking outside for a cigarette while she waited for her friends (and her father, who got held up at work) to arrive at the county social.

None of them had been hard to find. They'd all been caught quickly, and exonerated almost as fast due to a lack of physical evidence and the Fifth Amendment.

He knew what it had done to him. He considered

himself functionally insane. He held his job, paid his bills, socialized when the situation called for it (for a while, at least)...and obsessed every minute over bringing her back. He turned over every rock, followed every completely baseless lead, and stumbled upon a ritual with only untrustworthy anecdotal evidence to suggest its effectiveness. He moved her body under cover of night so he would have privacy to work in. The town, the dance...all nothing but legend.

Desperation made him a believer, and that was where Animal #1 had come in.

With him, Jarv was too angry. He cut too deep and too often, and Dahlia only came back for a few confused minutes before crumpling to the ground.

#2 was more successful, but, as Ms. Tynes had implied, the night had ended very early.

He needed practice.

The town offered him a nearly endless supply of subjects. It consisted, it seemed, of three types of citizen: grieving fathers, dead girls, and degenerates of every offense whose blood was their only worthy aspect. He didn't know who to thank for it, but he was grateful nonetheless.

They arrived at the grave, and he gently laid Dahlia down.

He shined the flashlight into the hole. Animal #3 had passed. Everything that Jarv had learned told him that it should have worked this time. He'd honed his skills to the point that they'd rival a professional surgeon's (or torturer's). The incantation was spot on, the cuts perfect, the sacrificed one of the men who'd taken the innocent life.

Ms. Tynes, bless her...her?...had shown him what

he was missing, and just when he was down to his last chance, too.

If he ever had any doubt about what he was doing, about his righteousness, it had been erased with a few words scrawled on his palm. This was what he was supposed to do.

One of the guilty must read.

He swapped the bodies out. He was equally as rough with #3 as he was gentle with Dahlia. He placed her within her casket, shut the lid, and filled it in. He threw the animal into his trunk and would dispose of him as he had the others, with absolutely no dignity or chance that they'd ever be found.

For the next twelve months, #4 had a guardian angel. He'd be shadowed. He'd be protected. He'd be *immortal*. Then, on the next anniversary of Dahlia's death, he'd die.

Dahlia would be back, no matter what it might cost Jarv, or anyone else.

And she would dance forever.

Sick Day

A man getting breakfast takeout. A daycare across town. A zombie outbreak. What could go wrong?

* * *

click

My name's Lucas Gallagher, and if you're listening to this, you've probably done a whole lot better than I did. It probably means that I failed myself and everyone I love miserably. But I want you to know that I tried. God, I tried.

I'd just dropped Nathan, my four-year-old son, off at daycare. It was my last day at work before taking a vacation for Christmas. I wouldn't be back until the 2nd…unless, I often joked with my coworkers, you believed the "end of the world" kooks. On the way to work, the grumbling in my stomach reminded me that I'd skipped breakfast, and it was time to rectify that. It was a crisp but clear December day, so I figured I'd park in the garage and take a quick walk to the café a few blocks down the road. Whether or not they had breakfast burritos seemed like the most important thing in the world at that moment.

I walked through the door; the tinkling of the bell added a nice touch to the café atmosphere. The owner's daughter was behind the counter, as she was every morning before her classes began. "Hey, Mr. G!"

"Hi, Aubrey. How's school going?"

"Ugh. But the good news is that we have burritos today!"

"You read my mind. Make it a double order, pretty please."

She winked at me. "Ten minutes."

I took the newspaper from the counter and flipped through the sports page. I was checking up on my fantasy football team when I heard a car crash outside. It was followed by a commotion that grew louder by the second. I thought I heard a few people screaming, and a few seconds later I was sure that it was more than a few.

I looked at Aubrey, who was, coincidentally, looking right back at me. We both turned to the front of the café, then back to each other. I assumed that her look of confusion was echoed in my own face. There was no logical reason for it. Collisions, sirens, angry yelling…all of these were commonplace in this town.

But this just felt different.

I took seven steps towards the door (seven steps exactly…it's odd the kind of details that stick with you) where I could see that a car had veered off the road and crashed into a convenience store. I saw two figures wrestling around on the ground while several other people seemed absolutely panicked. I had no idea why; it was just a car crash. Still, the behavior of the other people is what bothered me. I opened the door to give whatever help I could, even if it was just breaking up the fight. I'm not a small guy, and people tend to listen to me when I use my outdoor voice. I looked back at Aubrey and said, "Call the cops."

Aubrey didn't respond right away, and I didn't notice. I was focused on the task at hand when a man stumbled into the café, nearly bowling me over. He was covered in blood, and I was horrified to see that his left arm was missing below the elbow.

Then I got a good look at what used to be his face.

"Jesus Christ!" I was already removing my belt to form a makeshift tourniquet, and I just hoped to keep the poor bastard alive until real help arrived. I moved to help the mangled stranger, but he wandered right past me. He had to be in shock. I yelled, "Buddy, stop! You need help!" He didn't pay me any attention whatsoever, so I grabbed his shoulder and spun him around, determined to help this man whether or not he wanted it.

What I first saw in that face was the torn, bloody skin. It looked like someone had bitten off most of his left cheek, and a bit of his eye with it. There was a look of hopeless terror in his good eye, but that lasted for only a few more seconds, until it was replaced by something else.

Hunger.

With a terrible shriek, the man lunged at me, his jaws opening impossibly wide. Reflex took over, I dodged, and the man went sprawling well past me. "What the fuck's wrong with you?!?" was all I could think to say. It seemed appropriate.

He struggled to stand. His movements were clumsy and slow, but determined. I was rooted to the spot.

So was Aubrey. I already said that I'd forgotten all about her, right? I remember that she was standing with the phone pressed to her ear, mouth frozen in mid-syllable. She was terrified, and I wanted nothing more than to hustle her out of there and get her someplace safe.

I noticed too late where she was standing. The man shot his remaining arm out and pulled her to him, burying his face in her neck. He tore at her throat with his teeth like a wild animal, and Aubrey was only able to scream for a few seconds before a wet, gurgling sound took over. Her helpless eyes were locked on me.

I screamed, "Get off her!" and moved to help, though I knew she was already dead. I had been slow, far too slow. Still, I managed to kick the man aside. I heard a sickening crack as he landed awkwardly on his right arm. He was missing one arm and the other was broken, and that's the only reason I had time to tend to Aubrey. I tried to stop the spurting blood with nothing more than my hands, but the jets quickly diminished by degrees until the glint left her eyes and she was completely still. "Oh, I'm sorry, kid. I'm sorry."

As if on cue, her eyes snapped open. The ice blue eyes that had winked at me innocently countless times now held the same look as the crazy guy who'd just killed her. She leaned forward, her teeth gnashing. I started backing away, careful not to trip over anything, especially the lunatic who'd almost regained his feet, because I knew that would be the last mistake I'd ever make.

They seemed to be of a single mind as they came after me. Their movements were totally uncoordinated, and that was the only reason I made it out of the café alive. While they bumped into the counter and tables, I just ran.

Outside was total chaos. I thought the scene inside the café was bad, but it was multiplied tenfold out there, and it grew worse by the second. The already-narrow street was blocked off by a pile-up of smoking cars. Screams filled the air, and people were running everywhere. The ones who weren't currently running were either attacking or being attacked.

Hell had arrived.

I didn't care for these people right now. I couldn't help them. I had to get to Nathan. And Kate. That was all that mattered. That was everything.

So I ran. I dodged all manner of obstacle: wreckage, fire, corpses, and the arms of those who wanted me as their next meal. To be honest, I was scared shitless, but the fear worked for me. I didn't think, I couldn't think. I could only move. I had to get to my truck. If I couldn't, I was dead. It was that simple.

My pickup was only a block away now, and the coast looked, if not clear, at least passable. My adrenaline was pumping hard, and my senses were sharp enough to help me avoid the stray, well, I guess I finally realized that they were zombies, with relative ease. I had to avoid a few who'd either strayed to the second level of the garage or had turned there. I jumped into my truck and got into motion immediately. I had one purpose right now, and that was to get to my son. I had no idea how fast or how far this had spread already. All I knew is that the downtown buses had a stop at the daycare center. If someone had gotten infected on that bus.

I drove fast, slipping my seat belt on as I did. I flipped open my cell phone and dialed my wife's. She worked on the other side of town, so I'd have to get her second. Right now, my son needed me, and I knew that my wife would agree.

"C'mon, pick up, pick up!"

She did, on the second ring. "Hey, baby. What's

up?" She didn't know.

"I'm on my way to Nathan. Are you okay?"

"Why wouldn't I be okay? Is Nathan all right?"

"Listen to me. Are you inside your building?"

"Yes. What's going on?"

"Stay inside. Get behind every locked door you can." I paused, and decided to just come out with it. "Zombies."

"What? Are you drunk?"

"I'm not fucking around, Kate! Just listen to me! Tell everyone." I heard several popping noises over the phone. "What was that?"

"I'm headed to the window," Kate said. I heard movement, and then I heard my wife gasp. "Oh, my God."

"Kate?"

There was nothing.

"Kate!"

"There are…crazy people…out there. The police are shooting them, but they're not dropping." She paused as the reality sank in. "Nathan."

"I'm taking care of him, don't worry about him. Tell everyone to stay there. Lock every door. Barricade them. Find weapons. Wait for me. Do. Not. Leave. I can't do what I have to do if I'm worrying about you. Do you hear me, Kate?"

"Yeah, I just don't know how I."

"Don't think about it. I'm trying not to."

"Lucas…please keep Nathan safe. I love you."

"I love you. I'll see you soon."

I hung up, and that was the hardest thing I've ever had to do.

* * *

My worst fears were realized when I saw the overturned bus less than three hundred feet short of its stop at the Fun Time Daycare Center. The bus was smeared with what could only be blood, and there were a dozen dead bodies lying around, all of them at least partially eaten. I actually felt a slight sense of relief, because the more dead people there were, the less undead I'd have to contend with to get my son. I was ashamed of myself at that moment, but nothing else meant a goddamn thing to me. I'd deal with the guilt later, provided there was a later.

I pulled into the parking lot, reached under the rear seat, and pulled out the tire iron. It felt good in my hand. I hoped I wouldn't have to use it, but those hopes were dashed when I saw the wide open front door.

Panic set in, I had no hope of controlling it. I yelled, "Nathan!" I kept repeating my son's name, hoping it would act as a talisman, protecting him until rescue arrived. My rational mind knew that I should be silent and move slowly, but I just couldn't stop screaming. "Nathan!"

I ran straight to the preschool room. I encountered only one zombie there, wandering around the office. I knew her by name.

Her name was Miranda, and I spoke to her less than an hour before when I dropped him off.

Now, she was one of them. She came at me with a horrifying groan, arms outstretched and hands clenching at air. I gripped the tire iron with two hands and reared back like I was swinging a baseball bat. I wanted to hesitate, to give her a chance to be human, I

51

really did, but there was no thought but removing whatever stood between me and my boy. I felt soulless, but I swung with everything I had. It connected fully with her chest, and I heard ribs crack. The Miranda-thing staggered backwards, but soon resumed her course as if nothing had happened. I swung once more and connected with her face. Her cheekbone shattered and I knocked her back again. This time she tripped over a toy and fell down. I pressed my attack and brought the tire iron down in wide arcs until her head was a misshapen lump and she finally, mercifully, stopped moving.

I wiped her blood spatters from my face and looked around the room.

Five seconds later I had to fight the urge to vomit. There were several bloody, child-sized forms strewn about, forms that used to be children I'd seen five mornings a week for a couple of years now. It was…unimaginable.

Any one of them could have been Nathan.

I told myself he wasn't dead, that he couldn't be dead. I forced myself to look more closely. I tricked my brain into adopting a more clinical attitude, but that façade fell away almost as quickly as it appeared.

I couldn't tell. They were unrecognizable. I honestly didn't think I'd be able to tell if Nathan was there.

I leaned against the wall, crying and feeling defeated. I heard groaning and the shuffling feet of more zombies. I assumed it was the rest of the staff. I wanted them to come and finish me.

Then my eyes fell upon the area where the children kept their shoes.

Nathan's weren't there.

I looked at the feet of the dead children.

My little boy's Spider-Man shoes weren't on any of them.

My heart lifted, my focus returned. It was only a glimmer of hope, but it was enough. I wasn't going to give up on my son until he was in my arms or I was dead. Not one second earlier. I threw a bunch of toys near the doorway, making a minefield of sorts. I'd seen the things in action, and coordination wasn't their strong suit.

Four of the beasts entered the room and groaned in concert as soon as they saw me. They tripped and fell repeatedly over the toys, which enabled me to dance around and pick them off one by one. My plan was perfect, though I can't say the same about my execution. I had a scary moment when the last zombie actually tripped into me and bit down on my forearm. I hollered and kicked it away before bashing its head in. I checked my arm, wondering how long I had before I turned.

Luckily, my leather jacket had held, though I could see teeth imprints in the material. Good thing this is December and not June, or else I'd be one of them by now.

When I finished the last one, I started searching room by room. I considered it a perverse mercy that the staff had killed the children instead of turning them; I didn't know if I could kill a child, even an undead one.

I heard a muffled cry from behind a closet door in the room for one- and two-year-olds. It sounded too young to come from my son, but I had to check. I crept to the door, keenly aware that there was more than just the five staff members that I'd managed to dispatch. I put my head to the door and whispered, "Nathan? Is that you?"

I heard another stifled noise, so I raised my weapon in my right hand as I turned the handle with my left. I opened it slowly.

"Daddy!"

I scooped my son up in my arms and gave him a bear hug, breathing him in. I detected the faint scent of dried-up tears. Nothing had ever smelled so good to me. "Good soldier, good soldier." I didn't want to let him go, but now we needed to get to Kate. I put Nathan down and took his hand. "Let's go pal."

"Wait, Daddy. What about Carly?"

"Carly?" I remembered the child's cry that I'd heard. I walked back to the closet and moved aside several boxes. A little girl sat there, pacifier and all. I knew that I had just been presented a giant problem, but I didn't entertain the thought, even for a split-second, of leaving the girl behind. I grabbed a diaper bag and filled it with diapers and formula. I had no idea when we might see those again, if ever.

"She was scared, so we hid in here. Mommy always told me that if I got scared to hide and be quiet and you'd find me."

I felt a surge of pride in my boy. "See? Mommy was right." My thoughts were almost fully on Kate now. I had to get to her. I picked up Carly, who nestled into my arms immediately. "We have to go now, Nathan. Stay right behind me."

The trip back to the parking lot was uneventful, but once we got there, I discovered where the rest of the staff was. I peeked around a corner into the parking lot; they (and what had to the remaining bus passengers) were congregated around my truck, fascinated by the sound of the idling engine. I hadn't made a conscious decision to leave it running, but it was a good thing that I did. Now they had to be dealt with before we could go anywhere.

I knelt down with the girl still in my arms. "I have to do something so we can leave. Can you be a good soldier and take care of Carly for a minute?"

"Uh-huh."

"Take a seat, buddy." Nathan sat down, and accepted Carly into his lap. He wrapped his arms around her in a protective gesture.

"Stay here. I'll be right back."

I closed the door behind me and whistled. I got their attention.

* * *

Nathan sat in the passenger seat, Carly on his lap. The seatbelt was fastened across both of them. It definitely wasn't something the parenting groups would approve of, but I had no baby seat. I wasn't all that worried about getting a ticket.

Father and son hadn't said much since their escape from Fun Time. I thought that my son was blessed in that he had been shielded from most of the horrors while he had been stashed in his hiding place, and what he did see he couldn't fully comprehend.

I comprehended all of it, which is why I drove facing away from my passengers. I didn't want them to see my tears. I had to keep it together, even though I'd power-dialed Kate's phone ever since we left and had gotten no answer.

I wasn't going to give up on her. I always believed she was stronger than me, so if I was alive...

The ten-minute drive seemed to take forever, but we finally pulled into the lot of her office building.

Fifty yards away were the dozens, even hundreds, of zombies who had beaten us there. They surrounded the first-floor parking garage, and some were pounding the steel door that led to the stairwell. I had no idea if any had gotten inside, but I couldn't worry about that now.

My wife was in there somewhere. I looked at her office window, hoping to catch a glimpse, but there was no movement in her office.

I'd been noticed, but I had a little time before the shambling nightmares were a threat. I grabbed the tire iron...I felt vulnerable without it...and climbed on the roof to get a better view. After a minute or two, a plan popped into my head. I thought there was a pretty good chance that it might work. I hopped off the roof and used the iron to smash the passenger side view mirror to the ground, knowing that every inch would count. Nathan smiled at me through the window. The noise got the attention of some of the crowd, and they began to shuffle en masse in my direction. That actually worked to my advantage, because the less I had to deal with in the garage itself, the better the chance of success. I moved back to the driver's side, when something...a feeling that made the hairs on my neck rigid...made me look up to my wife's office. She was standing in the window, waving with both arms.

"Yes. Yes!" I yelled, not caring who, or what, heard me. More heads turned in my direction. I hopped into the cab, put my seat belt on, and honked the horn.

Still more came at me; there couldn't be more than a handful left in the garage itself. I took one last look upwards, and saw a large silhouette appear behind my wife.

"Oh, no. Nonononono! KATE!!!"

I watched in horror as Kate was yanked out of sight. I felt lifeless. I went through all of this, and she was taken from me less than two hundred feet from where I now sat. My eyes were glued to the window. I barely noticed when the first zombie reached the truck and began to claw at the window.

I screamed and pounded on the steering wheel. I knew I was scaring Nathan, and I think he begged me to stop. I didn't, I couldn't, and he started crying, which made Carly start crying, too. I didn't care. It was over. I was through. There was no point. I began to have insane thoughts that seemed saner by the second. I thought that smothering the two children would be the right thing to do. It was more merciful than letting them be eaten, or worse, get turned. I spared a thought that Carly's parents would someday understand and forgive me, if they were still alive. We were surrounded, and the noise was deafening. Nathan was screaming now, and the only intelligent thought I had, even when surrounded by a horde of flesh-eating creatures, was that I was a complete failure as a father.

I jumped as my cell phone beeped once.

A little envelope flashed on the screen. I opened it and actually began to laugh. My wife, who absolutely hates texting in general and text-speak in particular, had sent: "im ok.strwll clr.luv u bth."

I looked up to the window once more and saw her familiar form waving at me; she seemed to have an idea what I was planning, judging by her message. If you don't know, that's one of the most annoying parts of being married: the inability to have an original thought. You finish each other's sentences, you step on each other's jokes, you even know how they're going to argue a point before the other does.

It was anything but annoying then.

She was okay, and my needle went into the red.

I reached over and double-checked the kids' seatbelt. I hated that they had to be here for this, but there was no other option. I engaged the four-wheel drive and threw the truck into reverse. The zombies that were unfortunate enough to be directly behind me got crushed under the tires, and we got bounced around pretty good as we rolled over them. Sick as it sounds, I was flying so high at that moment that I was actually having fun. I got a little separation from the undead then slowed to a crawl, drawing as many of those bastards away from the building as I could, Pied Piper-style. That's when I grabbed my MP3 player and started this narrative.

Just in case.

I apologized to my son for scaring him, and I swear he sounded indignant when he said, "I wasn't scared, Daddy."

He really is a good soldier.

He's got this hopeful look in his eyes. I know what's on his mind.

I'd love to tell you more, but I'm out of time.

Someone else is waiting for us.

click

Tigers

*This is both the sequel (told from another
perspective, really) of "Sick Day" and a short story I
wrote specifically to help out my friend at Bare Naked
Bake Sale (http://www.indiegogo.com/Bare-Naked-
Bake-Sale). The stories in Justina Walford's fundraising
short story collection all start with some variation of:
"They're all gonna burn!" he/she yelled as he/she ran
naked into the kitchen. Just go with it.*

* * *

"They're all gonna burn!" I yelled to no one in
particular as I ran naked into the kitchen. I fumbled with
my pants, as I didn't want to actually be naked when I
ran into one of my coworkers. To be honest, I'm just
happy that I had the presence of mind to grab my pants
after I saw the bus careening into the parking lot
through the lightly-frosted glass of the men's room
window. Until then, the only thing on my mind had
been the last piece of cheesecake in the fridge. So help
me God, if anyone ate that thing...

Where was I? Oh, the kitchen.

My assistant, Tess, looked shocked as I entered,
whether at my demeanor or waist-up nudity I really
never had a chance to ask. "What, Del? What?"

"Call the cops! A bus just crashed into the lot!
It's burning!"

"Omigod!" She ran to the kitchen window and
looked down at the scene five stories below. I looked
over her shoulder, and almost didn't notice her perfume,

something sexy and spicy. Almost.

Then I got a better look at the scene. Somehow, it had gotten a lot worse in the few seconds that had passed between me getting ready for a racquetball date and unintentionally pressing the cute brunette against the window as I craned my neck to get a better look.

I'd already known that the bus was overturned, and that I'd seen flames burst into life. The fire must have spread incredibly fast, because the front half of it was engulfed in flames.

The people inside...the people...

...were walking around. Not all of them, I guessed. A crash that horrific, it would have been a miracle if no one died. As it was, more people were walking around than I would have bet on. A few of them just kind of...wandered aimlessly.

Oh, and some of those people were on fire, not that they appeared to care. I understand that shock can make people oblivious to a lot, but walking around on fire, with no more care than you or I would have for a minor sunburn?

Still, they needed my help. I pushed back from the window and into the rest of my Saturday skeleton crew, who had joined us at the window. Four more people at my back, two actually touching me, and I'd had no clue. "Jesus, Jimmy, move! Come on!" I ripped the fire extinguisher from its mounting next to the microwave. "Grab the other ones!" My team stood unmoving for a few seconds, still processing what they were seeing. My head was back in it, but I'd had a head start. "NOW!!!"

That got them moving. Jimmy, Elise, Carson, and Rick sprung into action. They each headed for a fire extinguisher while Tess frantically dialed the police.

The only one missing was Kate, my trusted second-in-command. If I'm being truthful with you, and I have no reason not to be, she's better than I am at this job, and I've felt like I've just been keeping the chair warm until she's ready to take over. I got where I got by collecting pelts. I'm a heartless killer. But I would have paid good money to be able to engender the loyalty that she does. I also would have given ten years off of my middle-aged life to make her mine for a night, but her husband's a really good guy, so I never tried anything. There's also the fact that she would have laughed in my face.

"Kate!" I yelled, as the five of us headed for the stairwell. "Where are you?" I was pretty sure I could hear her yelling a name. Nathan. Her son. She must have been talking to her husband, and she sounded close to panic.

She'll catch up, I though as we beat feet down the stairs.

Rick hit the door to the parking garage and flung it open. He held it as we raced to the bus. I sprinted with heroic intentions until I got a better look. My sprint turned into a jog turned into a feet-dragging.

The people on fire were still moving...somehow...only with a little more purpose.

That purpose?

The survivors of the bus. They crawled out or were dragged out by fellow survivors. They coughed as they sucked up the fresh air and expelled the toxic fumes of the inferno they'd been in.

Then the "walkers" fell on them and started tearing. This scene repeated itself over and over. The people in the bus had no idea what waited for them on the outside, not that they would have had a choice. Or would have believed it, anyway.

A patrol car had shown up, and the two overmatched officers fired at the things. They may as well have been firing blanks, and they were swallowed up.

I was at a dead stop. We all were, except for Carson. The situation had flipped a switch in the normally mild-mannered college whiz-kid. He was now all action. He reached the bus, pulled the pin on his extinguisher, and started spraying. He didn't make much headway; a smart kid like him would have known that he wouldn't, but A+ for effort.

Then he got noticed. He seemed to understand what was about to happen. He looked in our direction. He looked directly at me, his terror unable to deny even at that distance. I barely had time to yell out his name before they came at him. He tried to retreat, but it was closed off. He swung the extinguisher like a club and kept them off for a few seconds.

This broke our group inertia, for as long as it took for Kate's hand to fall on my shoulder and scare the shit out of me. "Del, we have to get inside!"

"What about the kid?" But I knew.

I knew.

My exchange with Kate took no more than five seconds, but Carson was already buried under a mass of flaming whatever-the-Hell. He screamed. He screamed a lot in a mercifully short time.

Then we got noticed, and they came. Worse, there was more of them. They'd recruited.

"Everybody back inside!"

We reversed ourselves, and Rick was the first to the door again. The circumstances were a lot more desperate for us this time, and he was the first one through, and I didn't blame him one bit. The five of us made it through the door in one piece but, unfortunately, so did they. We pounded up the stairs, yelling and screaming.

Elise stumbled and hit the stairs. Jimmy and I were closest to her, but our momentum carried us past her before her situation registered with us.

At least, I know that's what happened with me. I like to think the same was true for Jimmy.

I turned back to help her, but she was already being dragged backward by the fleetest of foot among the...

...zombies?

The zombies.

Dear Lord.

The rest of us made it to the fifth floor. Rick, ever the doorman, burst through, Kate and Jimmy next, me in the rear. One of those things got close enough to grab my shirt. I yelled and, without thinking, wheeled and punched it in the face. I felt its teeth dig into my knuckles and break under the blow. I didn't think I hurt it, but I did knock it back far enough to get away, but another one was bearing down now.

Jimmy screamed, "Come on, Del!" He left his relative safety to help me out. He pushed the second zombie down the stairs and its pinwheeling body clogged it momentarily, but not before he got a chunk taken out of his forearm for his trouble.

We slammed the door behind us.

"Motherfuck!" Jimmy yelled and cradled his

arm. It looked bad but not life-threatening.

"Block this door! Block this door!"

We grabbed whatever wasn't bolted down and wedged it against the door. It wasn't until after we were done that I remembered that it swung out into the stairwell, and unless those things knew how to pull a door open, what we'd done was pointless. Still, I felt a lot better.

Tess came over with some dish rags. "Here, let me see that." Jimmy sat down and showed her his arm. It was ugly. Jimmy grimaced as she cleaned it. Her hands worked on auto-pilot as she asked, "What happened out there?"

"I-I don't even know."

"It's not just here," Kate offered. "It's downtown, too."

"How do you know?" Jimmy asked.

"My husband just called me. He says it's a nightmare there. He's coming. After..."

"After what?"

She tried to speak, but was unable to.

I put a hand on her shoulder in what I hoped was a comforting gesture. "After he gets your son. And he will get your son. Don't you worry about that."

She didn't raise her head but nodded rapidly.

"What the fuck are we gonna do? We're trapped here!"

Rick said, "We do what we always do, Jimmy: Relax. Assess. Act."

"Relax...? This isn't a customer, and your motto doesn't mean shit, no offense." He got up and cursed again. "I gotta go wash this out. I probably have rabies now."

64

"Staff meeting in ten minutes!" I yelled, only partially joking. We needed to strategize.

"Yeah, yeah." He disappeared down the hall and into the men's room.

Tess held up her hands. They were streaked with Jimmy's blood. "Gross. I need to wash up, too."

Kate just walked away, and I didn't even have to ask where she was going: to my office to look for her husband's truck.

It was just Rick and me and the pounding at the barricaded door. He reached into the fridge and grabbed a few bottles. He handed me a soda that had "EVELYN" in inch-high block lettering on it. I didn't think she'd mind, so I cracked it and enjoyed the satisfying hiss as the gas released. It was something normal.

We drank in silence until Kate screamed.

I hauled ass into my office and saw Kate and Jimmy lying on the floor, locked in a struggle. She had her hands wrapped around his throat and her knees pinned against his chest, doing everything she could to keep his gnashing teeth away from her.

"Get him off me!!!"

"What the fuck are you doing, Jimmy?!?"

He turned his head and I saw the same insane-yet-vacant stare that I'd seen in the zombie I'd punched in the face. "Oh...oh, no..."

Jimmy forgot all about Kate, and that was good. But coming after me? Not so much.

I didn't think. My right hand acted on its own, grabbed the paperweight off of my desk, and met his temple with as much force as my serving arm could muster. There was a sickening thud and I felt the paperweight collapse part of Jimmy's skull. The blow knocked him off-balance, but that was only temporary.

Rick hit him with a chair.

I hit him with the paperweight again. And again.

He finally dropped and was still.

Tess came into the office and just stared. At Jimmy's body. At Rick and Kate. But, like Carson, mostly at me. I'm sure the blood- and brain-soaked paperweight had something to do with it.

Kate scrambled to her feet and started pounding on the window. "Lucas!!!" she yelled.

He apparently made it after all. Good on him. "Tess, he was...he was..."

Rick finished for me. "He turned into one of those things."

"Oh, my God, this is contagious?!?"

Kate had her phone to her ear and muttered something about the phones being down. She dialed again and said, "He's the only one of us who was bitten. That must have done it." She started to cry but choked it back. "I'm so sorry, Jim."

What she'd said made me look down at my hand. My knuckles had already started to scab over. No, I didn't get bitten, but was there really any difference between teeth hitting skin or skin hitting teeth?

I sighed. "We have to get you all out of here."

"And you," Tess said.

I held up my knuckles. "Not likely, sweetheart."

Kate grabbed my hand and inspected it closely. "Nonono, this is different. You didn't get bitten."

"Come on, Kate, you're smarter than that. Did you reach your husband?"

"Not yet. I think he saw Jimmy grab me. He must think the worst happened. He's just sitting there."

66

She checked her phone again. "Wait, the text went through." She ran back to the window. "He's moving! Wow, those things are like locusts. But he's...holy shit, he's crazy."

"What?"

"He's going for the stairwell."

He was crazy, but he was also their only hope. "Uhhhh, okay. Willing to bet everyone's life on it?"

"I know it. I know him."

"So there's your ride, folks. Here's my plan."

I told them. I cut off every protest. "I don't know how much time I have, but whatever it is, we're wasting it! Now cut the shit and do what I fucking tell you!"

That was it, the last thing I would ever say to my team. I reached into the refrigerator and grabbed a container. I walked to the elevator, all business. My skin felt like it was burning. It wasn't painful yet, but I had the feeling it soon would be. The skin around the bite was turning black. It was happening.

The elevator dinged at each floor, and I just hoped that a random zombie hadn't found its way on board. Otherwise, we were all dead. The doors opened, and the car was empty. I hit the button for eight and listened to the lame music for twenty seconds or so.

I stepped out and headed right to the stairwell door. I swung it open and cautiously made my way down the stairs until I saw the heads of the zombies at the door on the fifth floor. Not being the most creative guy I yelled, "Hey! Shitheads!" and got their attention.

They came for me, and I ran up to the roof. I hopped onto a fan housing and pulled myself up on top of the roof entrance. I laid down on my stomach as the zombies poured through the door and looked for me. If I stayed quiet, they might never notice me. But they might also lose interest and head back downstairs, and I would not let that happen. My time was done, but I could help the few friends I had left.

I opened the styrofoam container and looked at the piece of cheesecake. It got me thinking about an old parable. In it, a man was chased to the edge of a cliff by a hungry tiger. Lacking any other options, he jumped and grabbed onto a vine growing out of the cliff face. The tiger prowled a few feet above him. Far below him was another tiger. He heard a sound and saw that a mouse was nibbling on the vine. As it grew thinner and thinner, he plucked the sole strawberry, put it in his mouth, and let go. How sweet it tasted.

I got to my knees and surveyed my own situation. Below me, an eight-story drop. In front of me...tigers. Jumping would be the smart thing to do. A few seconds of terror followed by instant death. Quick.

But then I saw a loose piece of pipe that looked really sturdy.

I didn't think it would weigh much more than a racquetball racquet.

Before I knew what I was doing, I hopped down and grabbed the pipe. I cleared my throat, something I always did at the start of every meeting. Heads turned and eyes trained on me, as they always did. I climbed back on top of the stairwell before they could get to me. They surrounded me like 15-year-olds at a Bieber concert. They jumped and grabbed but came up with nothing but handfuls of air.

I heard screeching tires and saw a pickup truck racing away from the building. My eyes, still good after all these years, picked out several forms in the bed.

They waved, and I waved back.

My team.

I'd done what I set out to do, and there was really nothing left for me to prove.

I took a healthy bite of the cheesecake. Damn if it wasn't the best thing I ever tasted. I savored it, bite by bite, until it was gone.

I could jump, sure. The last thing I ever experience could have been the perfect taste.

But I've never really been one to pass up an opportunity to take a few more pelts.

Cupcakes

Dorothy can bake, and she made a special batch for a special occasion. This is the other story from the Bare Naked Bake Sale collection.

* * *

"They're going to burn!" she yelled, running naked into the kitchen. The insistent ding of the oven alarm chastised her one more time before she managed to hit the "Off" button. She grabbed a pot holder, opened the door, and pulled out the cupcakes in one smooth motion, honed by nearly 30 years of baking both for profit and fun. She stuck a toothpick in a random cupcake to test them, though she hadn't needed that beginner's trick for decades now. Truthfully, she probably didn't even need to set the alarm, but the oven had one, so no use taking the chance.

Especially not tonight. Tonight, everything had to be perfect. Setting the alarm today was a good decision, because she'd been lost in thought, distracted by the night's upcoming festivities. And she wouldn't have time for another batch before it was time to go.

She took them out and placed them with great care on the baking rack. She leaned close and breathed them in. *Always been my favorites,* she thought. *Chocolate isn't exactly the most creative recipe, but they're always a crowd-stopper. And this batch is something special.*

The phone rang. She picked up the handset and said, "Hello?"

"Hey, gorgeous."

"Jackson! I was just..." she looked down, now acutely aware of her own nakedness, "...I was just making myself pretty for our date." She returned to the bathroom and put her robe on.

"Too late," he laughed. "You're already there."

She felt herself blush. "Sweet talker. See you tonight."

"Can't wait. Bye."

The line went dead and she wasted a few moments grinning at herself in the mirror. She couldn't believe how, after all this time, everything was finally falling into place for her. The reconciliation with Jack was almost as unexpected as what had brought them back together in the first place. They thought alike so often it was scary. "You're a lucky girl," she said out loud. "Then again, it took a lot of hard work to get this lucky."

*   *   *

She knocked on the door for 4E. A young man answered. "Dorothy! I thought I smelled baked goods!"

"Hello, Justin," she replied. She offered the plate of cupcakes to him. "Choose your next victim."

Justin responded by cracking his knuckles, wiggling his fingers, and eventually selecting a cupcake. He'd done the same thing ever since she'd moved into the apartment complex and began baking for her neighbors. Every Friday night, without fail, for over two years. And he probably didn't even know it, but he picked the same position every time: second row, all the way to her right. "Look at the bottom," she teased.

He got a confused look on his face but did as he was told. He turned it upside down and laughed. He held it to her. On the bottom, written in permanent marker, was JUSTIN. "Now how'd you do that?"

"I don't just chat. I pay attention."

"I'm not surprised. Sometimes it seems like you know everything there is to know about us."

Now she laughed. "Everything really worth knowing, anyway."

He took a healthy bite. "Oh, God, this is awesome."

"Good night, Justin."

He mumbled through another mouthful and shut the door.

She continued her rounds as efficiently as ever, chit-chatting along the way. When the cupcakes were nearly gone, something odd happened: she ran into someone she didn't know. Dorothy guessed the woman was in her mid-30's. Pretty, even though she was dressed in sweats and looked kind of disheveled. She carried several boxes awkwardly and looked in danger of losing one. "Here, let me help you dear," Dorothy offered as she slid her basket over her forearm and grabbed the most precariously-balanced box. The look of relief was obvious, and Dorothy fell into step next to her for a few dozen feet.

"Oh, thank you so much. I'd shake your hand, but, uh..."

"Of course. Is this you?"

The woman looked at the door. "Yup. I have my key here somewhere..." She put another box down and fished in her pockets for a few seconds. "Eureka!" she cried, as she pulled out a single key on a chrome d-ring.

She led Dorothy into the apartment. "Please, just put that anywhere. Can I get you a water? That's all I have in my fridge."

Dorothy was a little more careful than instructed, and perched it safely on another, sturdier box. "No, thank you. At the risk of sounding obvious, just moving in?"

"Ha. Yes. I don't officially become a tenant until Sunday, but the super...what's his name...said I could get a jump on it. Nice guy."

"Yes, Murray's a nice fella." She added, almost as an afterthought, "He really minds his own business, too. That's a desirable trait in a landlord in a place like this."

"Hmmm, I bet." The last was said with a hint of real sadness, as if the woman knew that her new environment was in no way ideal for someone like her. "I've heard a little of the history. I don't know how much of it is true or not."

"Drugs, assaults, the occasional murder?"

"Well, yes, and the...thing with the girl..."

"What, the Jessica Tarver story? Too true, I'm afraid. Sexually assaulted and beaten to death by her degenerate boyfriend. Witnesses...and there were a lot, most everyone in this building, though some have moved on...say she died screaming for help. Help no one was willing to give her." Dorothy paused and took in the woman's horrified expression. "Our own Kitty Genovese. I say 'our' but that happened a year or two before I moved in. Still, community and all."

"That's awful."

"Just lock your door at night and you should be fine."

"That's comforting. I'm Janet, by the way."

"Dorothy. What brings you here?" She thought the pale skin where a wedding ring used to be told the tale, but she asked anyway.

"Divorce. And we didn't have a lot of money when we were together. Now? This is as good as I can do until something comes along. No offense."

"Please. I'm only here because I'm on a fixed income, dear."

"I hear that. Every extra dime I save for my son. No reason for him to have to suffer because my taste in men is atrocious." Janet took a long gulp of her water. "Wow, I'm starved. I forgot to pick anything up." Her eyes wandered to the remaining cupcakes.

Dorothy noticed and said, "I'm sorry, but these are all spoken for. It's a...tradition here." *You've only been here ten minutes. You haven't earned one of these yet, young lady.* "But give me a little bit, and I'll take care of you."

"That's okay. I didn't even know I was doing it. I have to hit the market anyway. Do you need anything?"

"No, thanks." She checked her watch. "Well, I have to be going. It was nice to meet you, Janet. I hope you enjoy it here, for as long as you stay, that is. For your sake, I hope it's not long."

"You and me both. Wait," she scribbled on a piece of torn cardboard and handed it to Dorothy, "...call me if you need anything. Or if you just want to watch trash TV."

The older woman nodded and slipped the number into her purse.

There was a soft click as the door closed, and Dorothy continued about her business. It wasn't long before she was finished. Instead of heading back to her apartment, she walked through the security door and to the street. The sun was just dropping below the horizon as she walked to her car, threw the baskets in the trunk, and headed to her date.

* * *

Jack greeted her with a hug and a slow, deliberate kiss. "It's so good to see you, baby. Everything go okay?"

"Sure did. A few people weren't home, but we'll have nothing but time for them. You have the tickets?"

"Of course. One last thing to take care of."

"No problems with that?"

He scoffed. "I had to call in a few favors to get the materials, but the rest was like riding a bike. You don't forget training like that."

He pulled out his phone and punched in a number. Dorothy fell into her old habit of people watching. It was something that she always loved to do, especially at airports. There was so much raw emotion here, and almost all of it positive, that it never failed to cheer her up.

Jack held his phone out to her. "Care to do the honors?"

She took the phone. Her finger hovered over the "Send" button. She paused, not because she had second thoughts, but because of the end of a daunting body of work that she'd undertaken almost entirely by herself. All of the neighborhood thugs, the endless information gathering, the pharmaceutical research, the crimes committed to get her hands on the occupancy records from four years ago, learning everything she could about every tenant in the damn building, discovering that there were myriad excuses but not a shred of remorse among them...

...and the Friday night baking. Having to bake for and then smile at the very people who were too uncaring or cowardly to lift a finger to help her daughter when she needed it most. Dear Jessica, who only lived there because she didn't want to take the money that her parents had gladly offered because she knew they'd needed it.

She'd done nothing to deserve that. Nothing.

Dorothy hit "End."

Jack furrowed his brow. "Something wrong?"

"No, just something else I forgot to do." She found the piece of cardboard and dialed the number. "Janet? Hi, this is Dorothy. I hate to ask this, but my car broke down. Can you come and get me? You're still at the market? Oh, that's lucky. Wait, it just started up. No, I'm sure I can get home. Sorry to bother you, Jes...Janet."

She hung up, entered another number, and dialed without hesitation this time. She made sure the call went through, then snapped the phone shut. "Now I'm ready." Jack grabbed her hand and they headed to the terminal.

* * *

Dorothy had the window seat. Jack could easily lean over her, if he wanted to.

He'd most likely want to.

Perhaps the most difficult piece of information

76

to get was finding out (without arousing suspicion, of course) which flights had a path that passed almost directly overhead the apartment building. The destination was secondary; the flight was the thing. She'd done it, and now she was blessed to see the huge pillar of smoke rising beneath them. The flashing red lights were everywhere, and she said a prayer for the firemen. She didn't want anything to happen to them, especially seeing as Jack would have rigged it to make it impossible to put out with water.

They were heroes.

They were nothing like the inhuman creatures that she'd been forced to call neighbor. She knew that a few of the people in the apartment had nothing to do with Jessica's murder, that they'd moved in after the fact, but that place was toxic, irredeemable. It was only a matter of time before they did something to warrant it (*Just look at me*, she thought).

But not Janet. She wasn't like them yet. She had time.

She thought of the last moments of those monsters, the drug coursing through their system, the taste of the cupcakes it had been hidden in still on their tongues. They'd be paralyzed, struggling for breath, but completely possessed of their wits. They'd feel it, feel every bit of it, just as Jessica had.

They're going to burn. She squeezed Jack's hand. *They're all going to burn.*

Terror by Text

I wrote this story while sitting on my deck, having a cigar. When I started it was light out, but dusk crept up without me noticing. This story creeped me out more than any other in the collection, though I'm fully aware that the title sucks.

* * *

ScaresYou: Well, I hope you're ready for this. I'm at the old Windy Meadows Sanitarium. Alone, as I promised. Go to my page to see a stock photo of the exterior. That was taken a long time ago. It's much creepier now.

ScaresYou: The sun just disappeared below the horizon. We have liftoff.

ScaresYou: Oh, and it looks like rain. How perfect is that?

ScaresYou @1HungLow: Good question. The load = 2 bright-ass LED flashlights, headlamp, lantern, cell phone (duh), extra batteries for everything, sandwiches, couple bottles of water, sleeping bag, latest SK book.

ScaresYou @dainbramaged: No gun, but I do have an unlicensed nuclear accelerator on my back. Hea-vy.

ScaresYou: In we go...

ScaresYou: Nice: RT@blockcocker When someone

asks if you're a god, you say yes!

ScaresYou: I should warn you that these "Ghostbusters" quotes could go on all night. If you haven't ever seen it, why are you reading me?

ScaresYou: Creaky door...cool. Forgetting about creaky door and letting it slam behind me...not cool.

ScaresYou RT@Robomop: Break out the backup underwear?

ScaresYou: Heh. It'll take more than that to make me shit my pants. Oh, damn...what if I actually have to take a crap tonight? How long before TP biodegrades, anyway?

ScaresYou: Moving on...dust everywhere, enough to leave footprints. So far, mine are the only ones. I see another set, I'm out. :-)

ScaresYou: When these places close, is it mandatory that someone be tasked with overturning gurneys in the hall and leaving a doll somewhere? Because I just saw both. #alternatecareerideas

ScaresYou: Spontaneous doll naming contest, and winner gets signed edition of whatever they want. Go.

ScaresYou: All of the "guest" rooms are open; I'll go to my grave wondering if that's creepier than closed doors or not.

ScaresYou @Darcy411: Yes, that was an absolutely awful choice of words. I have a real gift for that kind of stuff.

ScaresYou: There are bats here. Why wouldn't there be bats? I guess that means a lot less bugs, though. I'm Mr. Positive.

ScaresYou RT@corpsechristie: u hav the rite to remain in feer

ScaresYou: I love it when my fans get into character. Officer "Corpse" Christie, for those who might have only just discovered my work, was a cop (complete with illiterate killer personality) in one of my earlier novels.

ScaresYou: He had...issues.

ScaresYou: Spontaneous naming contest winner: "Raggedy Sybil." @ccdrummer4life, send your book choice and mailing address.

ScaresYou: Holy crap, I wish I could tell you how fast my heart is racing right now. A damn raccoon just skittered right in front of me.

ScaresYou: "Skitter" is what creatures do in a place like this, by the way. It's a law; I looked it up.

ScaresYou: Also, I just shut that door fast. Starve, you little bastard.

ScaresYou: I just checked, and I got some great video of

the raccoon. Oh, I'm taking some video here and there. Check the site in a few days.

ScaresYou: Found base camp. Infirmary 1. They still have beds. I'll be burning my sleeping bag tomorrow, though. Regretting not bringing hand sanitizer. Or a HAZMAT suit.

ScaresYou: Lunch break. I won't bore you with details unless I find the Madonna in my turkey sammich.

ScaresYou: I'm fine. Sorry for the lull. Tryptophan kicked in and I dozed. No Madonna, although my hands were covered in fucking ants when I woke up. #heebiejeebies and #washyourhands.

ScaresYou: Yes, folks, I know the turkey sleepy thing is a myth. I bend truth but make you feel like it's still real; it's what you pay me for. By the way, thanks again for that. It beats actually working.

ScaresYou: And this is how you go from amusing to creepy in no time. Relax, dude. RT@corpsechristie sleep good? u wont sleep agin 4 a long time

ScaresYou: Obviously another aspiring author. :-)

ScaresYou: Into the next circle...just leaving my shit here for now.

ScaresYou: Wow, this place is decrepit. I can hear it falling down around me. I mean that literally. At first I though the cracking sounds were just rain (which has intensified, by the way), then I saw pieces of the wall flake off.

ScaresYou @KarlawithaK: I'm man enough to admit that, yes, I'm a little freaked out. But I've also gotten like fifty more ideas to scare the piss out of you, so that makes it a win/win.

ScaresYou: For the record, I've gained 16 followers since I walked through the door. I also nuked one. You might be able to guess who that was. I have a pretty high tolerance for morbid talk, but even I have my limits.

ScaresYou: No, I won't RT them, you sickos. ;-) Believe me, I'm doing you a favor.

ScaresYou: I'll be honest. A thunderclap got me bad. And I'm now looking at a door labeled "Violent Patients Ward." I volunteered for this?

ScaresYou RT@NovelistJunior: As an aspiring writer, you're my hero for keeping up your spelling and punctuation under duress.

ScaresYou: Several other people have sent similar thoughts. It's automatic for me. It kind of has to be.

ScaresYou: Let me give all of you wannabe-pros a valuable tip. Writers don't "practice." Every damn word you write, Tweet, email, Facebook, text...it's always game time if you want to ever be legit.

ScaresYou: dont eva tlk lik dis, k?

ScaresYou: My wife knows that if I ever send a text to her that isn't capitalized, punctuated, etc. to call the cops, because something's wrong. True story. Ask her.

ScaresYou @CopyCatherine: No, I'm not stalling. As far as you know.

ScaresYou: I've been to multiple haunted sites, been alone in rooms with serial killers, been married twice...and this is by far the most uncomfortable I've ever been.

ScaresYou: Signal's crappy here, so let me know if you're getting these.

ScaresYou: Good to know. Thanks, everyone.

ScaresYou: More pics for the site.

ScaresYou: Bad things happened here, people.

ScaresYou RT@BarryTBarnes: If you feel lonely, you're right next to the converted TB ward. Approx. 10,000 ghosts to keep you company.

ScaresYou: Gee, thanks for that.

ScaresYou: Found something weird here. I know I saw the layout of this place online somewhere. Someone find it and tell me what's between rooms 18 and 20.

ScaresYou: Nothing, my ass. I just went into both of the rooms and there's a big space in between. The room walls are cement, but the wall outside is just plaster. Do I engage in my first B&E?

ScaresYou: Somehow I knew which way that question was going to go. Apparently, all of my readers are felons. Eat your heart out, Dan Brown!

ScaresYou: Fire axe, meet wall. Wall, fire axe. Hey, they're tearing this place down, anyway.

ScaresYou RT@nahtanoj: This is the most awesome thing ever. Better than Geraldo/Capone.

ScaresYou: Not a normal wall. It's almost a foot thick. Had to take a break. But I'm through. You haven't seen darkness until you've seen THIS darkness. Glad I brought all of these lights.

ScaresYou: I thought I lost this guy. RT@corpsechristie: u screwd up

ScaresYou: Okay, now I definitely got rid of him.

ScaresYou RT@domino1212: What's in the room already?!?

ScaresYou: Nothing yet. Can't see a thing. It's a LOT bigger than I thought it would be. The hole looks like it's fifty yards away. No sounds. No echoes when I yell, either. It's cold.

ScaresYou: How can there be wind in here?

ScaresYou: Jesus, this place is vast. The lights aren't hitting anything. They're just getting...swallowed up.

ScaresYou: I tripped over a shoe. A white nurse's shoe! You know what? I'm heading back to the nice, normal part of the haunted hospital. This isn't worth a broken leg or cave-in.

ScaresYou: Yes, of course I'm taking the shoe as a creepy souvenir.

ScaresYou: If I didn't know better, I'd say the wind was following me. I'm that creeped out. Glad to be rid of that room.

ScaresYou RT@corpsechristie: 2 late

ScaresYou: Okay, I didn't RT that.

ScaresYou RT@corpsechristie: u dint hav 2 im out now

ScaresYou: What the Hell is going on here? Did one of you hack my account?

ScaresYou @CarmenZ: No, I am definitely not fucking okay! DID ONE OF YOU HACK MY GODDAMN ACCOUNT?!?

ScaresYou RT@corpsechristie: i did but not n the way u think

ScaresYou: I swear to God, if I find out who's doing this, I'll put you under this place. That's a promise.

ScaresYou RT@corpsechristie: tuff guy! tuff guys hav the rite to remain in pain

ScaresYou @corpsechristie: Fuck off, you psycho.

ScaresYou RT@corpsechristie: nice shirt 2 bad its got a big mayo stain on it now

ScaresYou: This prick can see me somehow. I'm outta here.

ScaresYou: Back in the infirmary. My shit's gone. He's here. Someone please call the cops. I'm not getting through. I'M NOT KIDDING. HELP ME.

ScaresYou RT@corpsechristie: u hav the rite to remain bleedin

ScaresYou: Someone please tell me the cops are on their way!

ScaresYou RT@corpsechristie: u hav the rite to remain screeming

ScaresYou: I see headlights. Thank you, thank you!

ScaresYou: Had a bad feeling and hid. Hear footsteps.

ScaresYou: Cop at the entryway. Lord, I recognize him. I created him.

ScaresYou: Freaking out. Not hanging around anymore. No place to go but back in. Send help. Please.

ScaresYou: Back at the hidden room. Remember how huge it is. Maybe lose him in here. Don't want to go back in.

ScaresYou: Yelling...gunshot...laughing. Footsteps echoing. Can't figure out where they're coming from.

ScaresYou: No choice. Going in. Room between 18 and 20. REMEMBER THAT.

ScaresYou RT@corpsechristie: u hav the rite to remain in custedy 4evr

ScaresYou RT@jabbathehuffer: You okay, dude?

ScaresYou RT@tammycakes: You there?

ScaresYou RT@tapout247: I'm calling the cops again!

ScaresYou RT@liquorupfront: Damn it, say something!

ScaresYou: im fine thx talk 2 ya l8r

How Many Years of Bad Luck Am I Up To, Anyway?

At 4:15 am Eastern Standard Time, every mirror ever made by the Charon & Niflheim Glass Company exploded. There were scores of mostly minor injuries, a few more serious ones, but no fatalities. It wasn't immediately a big news story, as it took time for people to talk about the weird thing that happened to them that day.

A security guard by the name of Carver Cole was responsible, but he's pretty sure that everyone would forgive him, seeing as he probably saved all of their lives.

* * *

Carver's old boss hadn't quite reached the point of begging. "We've been contracted to watch his business and estate while the vultures...I meant, heirs...duke it out. It seems that none of them trust the others to not lift stuff.

"Good for you guys."

"Come on, dude, I'm in a bind. There's no one else available to fill those shifts. I need you. Just like old times."

"I always liked you, Jimmy, but the old times sucked," Carver countered. "You know I hated that job."

"You couldn't use a little extra cash? It's almost track season."

Carver made a non-committal grunt.

"Easy work."

"I don't think..."

"And I'll give you supervisor pay."

Carver wasn't destitute. The warehouse job paid decently, but who couldn't use a little extra money? "All right, all right."

"You are the king, CC."

Carver laughed. "Put that on my tombstone." He hung up, grabbed a beer, and started rooting through his closet. He was right; he still had a few uniforms.

* * *

Carver had quickly gotten bored, and that's why he was in an unlit storeroom way off of his appointed rounds. He'd felt a strange attraction to this room and had bypassed several other more interesting rooms in favor of it. The room was understandably full of mirrors, a funhouse in its own right. Some of them were covered, others were not. As he moved around, touching here and there, his multiple images gave the illusion that the room itself was fluid.

The company's founder, Heinrich Niflheim, or "Niffy," as he was known to everyone, albeit behind his slightly crooked back, was dead three months now. Judging by the stories he'd heard, Carver thought that was a pretty good thing. Mysterious deaths in his family, dabbling in the occult, adding some of his own blood to the stain applied to each and every mirror; they had sounded like tall tales at first.

Then Carver saw the portrait and got an actual chill.

"That is one creepy-lookin' bastard," he said to the empty room. "Damn, you've got me whistling past the graveyard, wrinkles."

Even though Carver knew better, he thought the gaunt man seemed to be staring at something. Carver followed the inanimate gaze across the room.

"Goddammit," he muttered as the beam of light reflected off of the mirror and straight into his eyes. He blinked the stars away and refocused. He moved the light off to the side and used the beam's spill to look again.

Niflheim's face looked out from the mirror. Carver yelped and took a step back, then let out a relieved laugh. Someone had, maybe unintentionally, set the portrait directly across from the mirror.

"A-hole," Carver muttered. "Scared the holy Hell out of me."

His heart rate dropped back to normal, and he reexamined the mirror. There was a small etching in the top right corner: a stylized "HN." Carver had noticed the same maker's mark on each of the mirrors in the entire building. There was a small plaque on the bottom, as well. Carver wiped away the thin layer of dust out of habit.

"Let's see...'Reflections are but another aspect of a man, and need only an invitation and an anchor to open the pathways between worlds.'" He leaned in close and addressed the reflection. "Well, that's some pretty deep stuff, Niffy my friend. I'm glad that I never worked for you when you were alive."

Carver was about to say more, but he had an epiphany just then.

In order to read the inscription, he had moved to a position directly in front of the mirror. The portrait was behind him. There should be no reflection.

And the reflection-that-shouldn't-be smiled.

"What. The. F-?"

A hand and forearm shot out of the mirror and seized Carver by the throat. He gasped and instinctively knocked it away. The jagged fingernails left superficial gouges on his neck. He backed up, feeling absolute terror for the first time in his life. "Ohmygodohmygodohmygod..." came out of his mouth, but his sole thought was, *People can't instantly go insane, can they?* The arm that extended farther and farther out of the mirror suggested that yes, they could.

He retreated until his butt hit a collection of mirrors leaning against the wall. Carver had a death grip on his flashlight. The circle of light it cast showcased an arm that was fully extended to the shoulder, where it seemed to be stalled. The arm flopped side-to-side and the fingers opened and closed. It seemed to be feeling around for something. In the background, Niffy's face was distorted and flattened, pressed up against the glass and unable to advance.

Carver felt a searing pain in his thigh and screamed. He felt himself being pulled backward, and instinctively struck downward with the heavy flashlight several times. He was vaguely aware that the protruding arm from the mirror had disappeared from its original home and now reached for him from a different mirror. He violently battered whatever thing held him until he heard a crack. He struck again, heard a splintering sound, and yanked free. He turned and fled from the storeroom, barely dodging Niflheim's arm yet again.

He hit the long, narrow hallway and sprinted as fast as his wounded leg would allow. It hurt, and his pants leg was already soaked with blood, but he didn't think it was threatening. Even if it had been, he'd take the risk.

The corridor was lined with mirrors of various sizes and models. As he ran, they mirrors gave birth to appendages both human-like and not even close to human. Feathers, fur, scales...it was a gallery taken straight from a nightmare. They ended in fingers, or spikes, or hooves, or talons.

The only thing that Carver cared about at the moment is that they were all just a few inches shy of taking him down. He ducked, he slid, he dodged, he leapt, he did whatever he could to avoid it, because he knew that, if just one of them caught him, he was dead.

He approached the corner and risked a look behind him. A blur (he thought it had to be Niffy) jumped from mirror to mirror in pursuit. Carver turned into the next corridor blindly and got clotheslined by a humongous hair-covered arm. His legs flew out from under him and he hit the floor. This arm was long enough to reach him on the ground, and it hauled him to his feet.

Niffy caught up to him and took up residence in the mirror closest to him. The arm extended again and, this time, got a good grip on Carver's wrist. Carver expected to be dragged into the mirror, but quite the opposite happened. Sasquatch held him in place as Niffy used Carver to pull himself out of the mirror.

An anchor. I'm his anchor.

Carver struggled to break free of just one of them, but the leg wound and the hard hit he took were doing a number on him. Niffy had freed himself up to his chin, a triumphant sneer dominating his face.

Carver heard a roar of pain from Sasquatch. It

released him, and Carver could see why: there was a fire axe buried deep in its forearm. Carver seized the opportunity and punched Niflheim in the face. He shrieked and released Carver's arm. He snapped back into the mirror like a rubber band.

Carver saw his savior. "Louis!"

The janitor grabbed Carver and helped him down the hall. The onslaught seemed to have slowed down with Niflheim's temporary failure. Carver supposed that they were regrouping and the second assault would be even worse.

"What the Hell was that, CC?"

"Just get us outside and I'll tell you!"

Louis wasn't satisfied with the pace that Carver's injured leg dictated, so he draped an arm over his shoulder and practically carried Carver outside. They made it to the front lawn and collapsed.

"Thanks......saved...my life..."

"No...problem...you got a..hook...in your leg..."

Carver felt for his wound. Louis was right, except that it wasn't a hook, but a talon dug into his flesh. Carver had hurt one of those things.

"C'mon," Louis said as he helped Carver to his feet, "my place is right down the street. Carolyn can help me get you fixed up, and then you can explain to me what the Christ I just saw."

* * *

Carolyn had patched him up pretty well, and Carver had a giant souvenir monster hook to show for it. Louis brought Scotch, and Carver downed it in five quick swallows. Even high-end Scotch (which this wasn't) would burn like a son of a bitch a throat going down that quickly. Still, he felt pretty good in the twenty seconds or so before he noticed the "HN" on the large oval dressing mirror in the bedroom.

Carver's heart sank, and he knew that this was going to go bad quickly. He saw movement in the mirror. It was only a small circle. A pinpoint, really. But it grew larger in diameter by the second.

It was coming at him. Carver froze.

Carolyn picked up on the concern on Carver's face. "CC? What is it, sweet-?"

Carver pushed Louis aside as roughly as he could and tackled Carolyn to the floor in the opposite direction. Carolyn screamed and he felt a stabbing pain in his shoulder. He looked down and saw that the two of them were linked by the same immense needle-like appendage that had penetrated both of their shoulders. Veiny sinew trailed behind it and back into the mirror. Louis was screaming for his wife, but Carver was focused on the mirror. On cue, a withered hand broke the surface and grasped the sinew. Then the other appeared, and Niflheim began a slow but sure hand-over-hand entrance back into his world.

Carver tried to pull out the needle, but the searing pain told him it was barbed, and there was only one way for it to come out.

"Cut it! Cut it!"

Louis looked around frantically. "With what?!?"

"I don't know!!! Get a knife or something!!!"

Carolyn, apparently not satisfied with the progress of their dialogue, offered, "MAYBE YOU COULD TRY THAT GIANT RAZOR SHARP HOOK I JUST PULLED OUT OF A LEG!!!"

Louis grabbed the hook and began sawing through the flesh. He broke through and Niflheim, again, snapped back into the mirror. This time, someone was too close. Niflheim's hands wrapped around Louis' neck and the janitor's screams trailed off as he was pulled into the reflection and disappeared.

"LOUIS!" They screamed in unison.

Carver tried to get to his feet, but they were still anchored together. Carolyn was thrashing on the floor, screaming for her husband, and doing untold damage to both of them. He locked both of his palms around her face and held her still. he tried to speak as calmly as possible. "I'll get him back. I promise. I owe him. But you need to hold still." he repeated himself several times before she understood. "Okay, are you ready? This'll hurt."

Her tears were flowing freely, but she nodded. Carver put his hand flat on her chest and pushed her away from him. He could feel the barbs digging into his skin, but he only needed a few inches of separation. He gritted his teeth and pushed harder. Carolyn let out a hiss, but was a trooper. When he'd gained enough room, Carver grabbed the needle with his other hand and held it still while he freed Carolyn. The needle came free from her flesh with a wet sound. The pain made her eyes roll back in her head and she passed out, but they were separated. He clapped a hand to her shoulder and she bled...a lot...but it didn't look arterial.

"Aw, dammit, dammit...that's two holes now..." He picked the mirror up and was about to smash it against the bedpost. He didn't know if that would stop Niflheim, but it was worth a shot. Then a realization washed over him. *He doesn't have to come for me anymore. All he has to do is wait for me to come for Louis.*

And I will.

He had a plan. It wasn't even a terrible plan; it was insane. But it was more than he had now.

Carolyn was still out cold. Carver scooped her up and put her on the bed. He was pretty sure she'd be okay, but he wasn't about to take any chances. He picked up the handset by the bed and called 911. He kissed her forehead, whispered, "I'll get him back, or die trying," and went hunting for some car keys.

* * *

As he'd expected, his return trip to the store room at Charon & Niflheim was uneventful.

That didn't stop him from smashing every mirror in the store room, save for the one that had started it all. They'd started to look too much like doors into Hell. Or, worse...out of it.

He mentally calculated the wraith's reach, doubled it, and stood there.

The dead face floated up to the surface of the mirror once more.

"I propose a trade. I'll take your hand willingly. But you have to give me Louis first."

The head shook side-to-side.

"Come on, really? I can't run forever. I don't want to live in a cave. Just give me Louis. Then, I'm your...whatever. If you don't, I throw a sheet over you, stuff you in a trunk, and take my chances. You'll eventually get me, I don't doubt it, but I might make you wait a long time."

96

Carver made a lot of assumptions then, the biggest of which was believing that he was the only one that could bring Niflheim back.

Niflheim made a pointing gesture at the inscription, and Carver knew he'd guessed right. He moved closer and read the inscription again. Only a few seconds passed before a hand appeared. Even though he'd been expecting it, Carver nearly jumped out of his skin.

This hand had olive skin, and Carver grabbed it. He set his feet and pulled with everything he had.

The mirror made no sound at all as it regurgitated Louis. The two men tumbled to the floor.

Louis crabwalked away from the mirror in terror. "What the shit was that, CC?!?"

Carver actually laughed. "Hell if I know, Louis. Hell if I know."

"Why did he give me up?"

Carver looked back at the mirror. Niflheim was growing impatient that his offered hand had yet to be taken. "I made a deal."

"No, no, no...what I saw...you can't let them in here..."

"I made a deal."

"You can run!"

He could, Carver knew. If he was careful, if he packed that Godforsaken mirror far away, was careful to avoid any of the mirrors made by Niflheim...

...but they made so many. The company had begun with dressing mirrors, but had expanded over the years to include mirrors of all sorts. Cars, commercial...one day, Carver might walk by a building made of those mirrored panels and Niflheim would be free.

Even if he stayed in the middle of nowhere...forever...someone else would find the mirror. It had called to him; it would call to someone else eventually.

"Hey, Lou?" Carver said. "I'm sorry I dragged you into this. Tell Carolyn for me, will ya?"

"I'm not gonna let..." Those were the words that Louis got out before Carver shoved him out of the room and locked the door.

He ignored the yells and pounding and grabbed Niflheim's hand. Niflheim wasted no time and pulled himself up Carver's arm. He was about halfway out, and his face was no more than a foot from Carver's. His grip was strong. There was no way Carver could throw him off this time, even if he'd wanted to.

"There we go," Carver said. "I took your hand. Just like I said."

Then Carver smiled.

Niflheim, who had been smiling, looked confused.

Carver screamed and leapt, taking them both back into the mirror.

*   *   *

Jimmy Kane grumbled through his rounds. He couldn't believe that a reliable guy like Cole had left him high and dry like that. And trashed the storeroom, to boot! And here Kane was, filling in for him.

He walked several dozen feet past the storeroom door, then stopped. The back of his neck tickled, and he felt like he was forgetting something. He pivoted and walked back. He swiped his ID badge and walked inside.

The sole object in the room now was the large, ornate mirror. The Puerto Rican maintenance guy had personally removed everything that Cole had busted. The guy had been working the night that Cole ghosted, and Jimmy tried to ask him a few questions. The janitor had either deflected each question or just gone silent.

He knew something, but he wasn't telling.

Jimmy checked his refection in the mirror. The gray at his temples was still mostly under control, provided he kept his hair closely cropped. He thought he looked better than usual. Women had good hair days, so why couldn't a guy have handsome days?

He spied the plaque and, due to nothing more than habit, read it out loud.

The mirror grabbed him around the shoulders and wouldn't let go. He screamed and tried to break free, but the grip was steel.

The mirror had a voice. "Christ, Jimmy, don't let go!!!"

"Cole?!?"

"SHUT UP AND PULL YOU LAZY BASTARD!!!"

Jimmy either trusted Carver's orders or just wanted to get away from the mirror, but the result was the same. Cole managed to get one leg free, braced his foot on the frame, and shoved himself to freedom.

Jimmy tried to extricate himself from under his employee, but Carver covered his head with his arms and yelled, "Stay down!"

The mirror exploded with such force that shards embedded themselves into the drywall. Cole and Jimmy were low enough to avoid any major damage, though they both took superficial cuts to the head.

The room fell silent.

Carver pushed himself to his feet, then helped a thoroughly shellshocked Jimmy to his. Carver dusted off the man's security jacket and straightened his badge and whistle. "Thanks, Jimmy. I knew I could count on you."

"CC...what..."

"By the way, I quit." Carver took a long look at Jimmy. The man would recover, but right now he wasn't in good shape. Carver unzipped the jacket and slid it from his boss' shoulders. He put it on. It was tight in the shoulders and loose in the gut, but he only had to keep it on for three hours or so. "Tomorrow."

* * *

I wanted to leave you with a more upbeat ending, so allow me to introduce you to Carver Cole. I didn't know it when I started this story, but you'll be seeing him again in a full-length novel sometime in the future. I can't tell you what it's about, but it will involve lots of clowns.

I also thought this story would lend itself pretty well to a reader contest, so here goes: just tell me what you think happened during Carver Cole's time in the looking glass. Send your explanation to the email address found at http://dandewittfiction.blogspot.com/p/social.html. The best two or three that I read by the end of the year will receive some cool bonus stuff. I might even see my way to giving you an advance copy of something.

Orpheus

The Rookie

He didn't want to turn the corner. He didn't know what was ahead of him, but the only thing that was worse than that was that he had no idea what might be behind him. That thought served to overcome his fear, albeit temporarily, but long enough to decide to move ahead.

He raised his pistol, remembering his training that seemed to have taken place a lifetime ago. He took a series of quick, shallow breaths, calming himself the best he could under the circumstances. He was tired, alone, and scared out of his mind, but he was taking that corner now. He mouthed a silent battle cry and moved quickly to the door on the opposite side of the hall. It was slightly ajar, and he pushed it open with his shoulder, taking care that it didn't bang against the wall as it swung open. He stepped to his left, out of the doorway but not moving any further into the room, either. Despite the increasing dimness, he didn't need his flashlight to see that the room was empty and theoretically safe.

He clicked the door shut quietly and leaned against it. He released the breath that he hadn't realized he'd been holding and raised his flashlight. He swept it across what appeared to be a sitting room or a study in a slow arc, looking for anything that was both useful and portable. He didn't immediately see anything that fit that description, but there was an old-fashioned rolltop desk in the corner that might hold a treasure or two.

He moved to the desk, double- and triple-checking that he was really alone. He rolled it up and found nothing but basic supplies: paper, pens, a stapler, rubber bands, and some index cards. He grabbed the rubber bands and, as an afterthought, the index cards. *Those could come in handy for marking, at least.* He started rifling through the drawers, not coming up with much, until the second-to-last drawer.

Jackpot, he thought, and he grabbed the several unopened packages of batteries that were there for the taking. He decided that there was nothing else worth weighing him down, so he moved to leave. He put his ear to the door and listened for sounds. He wished that the door had something as simple as a peephole, but he didn't think there was anything out there. He opened the door, looked both ways like a kid crossing the street would, and continued down the hallway.

He heard a noise behind him and froze in his tracks. He spun around and saw one of the things at the end of the corridor. It must have rounded the corner just after he'd figured it to be safe. It still had its back to him, and he had plenty of time to deal with it. He raised his pistol and fired. The report was loud in the hall, but his aim was flawless, and the round hit it in the face. The thing moved a few more steps before realizing that it was dead. It fell to the ground, lying still for the second and last time.

I'm such a bada- was all he could manage to think before another noise, much closer this time, sounded in his ears. He barely had time to register that before a hand gripped his shoulder and tried to pull him closer.

"Shitshit!"

He shot his left arm behind him. When he made contact with the thing's chest, he pushed it away with a grunt. Its grip was broken and he got a bit of separation, but it moved to close the gap. This one was fast, and he was unable to get off a head shot, so he settled for several in its chest. The slugs knocked it backward, but it came for him again. This time he steadied his weapon with both hands and squeezed off two more rounds, the second taking the thing in the top of the head.

Two more appeared at the opposite end of the long hallway, attracted by the commotion. These two moved almost normally, and were in a near-sprint after him.

Sprinters. Figures.

Still, he knew that he had enough time.

And I have nine rounds. I'm okay.

He fired two more shots, the first in the neck. The second shot was fatal, hitting it almost perfectly between the eyes. He adjusted his aim to dispatch the second one and pulled the trigger.

The hammer fell on an empty cylinder. He fired again, but he was either jammed or out.

I can't be out. This is a 15-round magazine!

He felt around his waist for a spare magazine and came up with nothing. He realized what had happened, and broke into a run away from his pursuer. His heart was pounding as he tried to find something to put between him and the thing to buy him enough time to figure something out. The hallway was lined with doors, but if he guessed wrong and chose one that was locked it would be all over. He wouldn't have time for a second guess.

Then he saw the door to the stairwell. Above it was a red sign that said "EXIT" and it had a welcome crashbar lock release on it.

I can blow through that and catch my breath, at least.

He did just that. He slammed the door shut behind him and sat down with his back to it. He braced his legs against the handrail and prepared for the impact. It was more violent than he anticipated, but the door held closed. He heard a rapid flurry of pounding against the door for several minutes, but it began to wane quickly.

All I have to do is wait it out for a little while.

He heard a sound that made his heart drop. He was on the third floor, and the door to the stairwell was definitely secure. What he'd heard was the second floor door being opened and slamming shut. He was trapped between the thing behind him and whatever just came through the door. He didn't know what to do.

Please be Shufflers. Maybe they'll just fall down the stairs. Even if they don't, I can deal with a couple of Shufflers hand-to-hand if I have to. I'm okay.

They weren't Shufflers. They were Sprinters. Two of them. And they knew he was there. He grabbed his expandable baton from his hip and extended it with a metallic click.

I can do this!

He stood up to confront them and adopted a fighting stance. He raised the baton to strike, when the door behind him opened. He'd forgotten all about that one. It fell on top of him. He tried to strike its head with the baton, but he had no angle or leverage. Its face moved towards his throat with a hungry sneer.

105

One of the second-floor Sprinters had reached him on the landing. It stared down at him, head shaking in disapproval. It pulled off its mask and drawled, "Now what did y'all learn today, bait?"

* * *

Tim Driscoll kept arguing, but with less conviction every time. "All I'm saying is that it's bullshit that you guys messed with my gear. I would've..."

The man next to him said, "Just zip it, bait." Though he was roughly the same age as Tim, if that, he spoke with much greater authority that made him sound a lot older. Tim supposed that the man, known as Fish to his squadmates, had seen enough to age him. "You should've checked your load. Ain't no one's fault but your own." He looked to the locker across from him and the lanky Southerner sitting in front of it. "Tell him, Mutt."

Mutt didn't immediately say anything. He took his time hanging his jumpsuit in his locker and smoothing his hair. The masks that they wore to protect their faces from the air pistols were effective, but too tight for his tastes. Mutt slammed the door firmly and faced the other two men. "Fish's right, kid. You should always be checking your weapons, ammo, and gear. Always. Yeah, we screwed with it this time for the training, but out there you can drop a mag, forget how many rounds you have left in your piece, have dead batteries in your flash...just check your gear from now on."

"Got it."

Fish chimed in, "Always."

"Yeah, I got it."

The locker room door opened, and a stocky black man walked in. He nodded. "Fellas."

They returned the nod.

"Bait, the boss wants to see you. Now." To emphasize his point, he held the door wide open.

"I reckon you better hurry," Mutt said. Then he spoke directly to Fish. "Let's go grab a drink or six."

"I'm in. Sam?"

"Yeah. I'll grab some stogies from my stash. I'll meet you in a few." He got an impatient look on his face. "Now, bait."

"I'm coming, I'm coming." He shoved his gear into his locker and grabbed his lock. He paused, opened the door once more, and checked his gear. "Give it."

Fish laughed and produced a magazine from behind his back. "You're learning already!" Tim took it and put it away. This time he put the lock on. He followed Sam out of the room.

Fish finished lacing up his boots and asked, "What do you think, Mutt?"

Mutt considered the question, "I dunno yet. I'll wait and see what the boss thinks."

* * *

The walkie chirped in Sam's hand. "Yup, I got him." He looked at Tim. "You ready?"

Tim looked around. "For what?"

"To meet the man on the roof. Take the stairs. And take these with you." He handed the younger man two metal tubes. "You have sixty seconds starting right..."

"That's ten flights!"

"...now." Tim didn't move for a second or two.

"You really don't want to keep him waiting, bait."

Tim broke into a dead sprint and was on the roof with three seconds to spare.

* * *

Tim had to catch his breath for a few seconds. Hands on his knees, he surveyed the roof. There was no artificial light up here, but the moon was nearly full and the night was cloudless, making any man-made light sources unnecessary. His eyes adjusted quickly, and he saw a large outline silhouetted against the night sky.

Orpheus, he thought, and gulped involuntarily. "Sir?"

"Come here and tell me what you see," was the reply.

Tim did as he was told. He stood next to his commander and peered down on the city. He saw pockets of light here and there. He could make out occasional bursts of movement. His overall impression was of an eerie serenity, and he said as much. "Quiet, sir. Peace. But I'm a poet at heart."

"What do you think you'd see in the daylight?

Tim knew firsthand what was down there. "Hell."

"Know what I see?"

"No, sir."

"I see the same things that you do, but I have the benefit of experience, if you can call it that, to be able to see even further. I used to see survivors; I used to see hope. Now I see a place that's almost entirely bereft of it." With no additional segue, Orpheus said, "Your dry run went pretty well, all things considered. You showed good movement, a sense of what was worth taking, and a willingness to engage hand-to-hand, if necessary."

"Thank you."

"What did you do wrong?"

Tim had thought about this during his run up the stairs, and he thought he knew the answer. Everything was going well until he shot that first zombie (which had actually been Orpheus himself, though Tim had no way of knowing that). "I engaged when I didn't have to. I could have avoided the Shuffler and gone about my way without alerting the Sprinter."

"We want to be shadows. We're precise, quiet, surgical. Our nickname's kind of cheesy, but it fits what we do. We avoid engagement whenever possible. The training, such as it is, is just a taste of how bad it can get and how quickly it can get there. Understood?"

"Yes, sir."

"Why do you want this?"

"I'm sorry?"

"Why would a young kid like you want to march willingly into that mess?"

Tim paused. He knew what he wanted to get across, but he wanted to get the words right. "Someone saved my ass down there. I rolled my ankle pretty bad, and I was limping to an extraction. An armored car was all it was, really. A couple of Sprinters were on my ass. There was no way I was going to make it. Then a man and woman came out of nowhere and held them off long enough for me to get in the armored car. They were a couple, I think. Had to be."

"Were?"

"She made it to safety. He was about to...I mean, he was right there...and he misjudged his jump. It was just enough for the first Sprinter to catch up. The woman jumped out and fought like a demon to save the guy. I expected the eight or so other people to help them, but we drove away. I yelled to the driver to wait, but he just yelled that they'd already waited once for me and floored it. I almost rolled out the open door when he did that. Imagine how stupid that would have been."

The older man nodded as if he'd seen the same kind of thing, then turned his gaze to Tim's face. He was almost entirely in shadow, but Tim still felt like he was getting an x-ray. "And?"

"And I want to pay them back, sir. I'll never know who they are, but I want to do something with the second chance they gave me."

That x-ray feeling intensified, and Tim knew that this man in front of him was scanning for bullshit.

"Good. Your motives are pure enough to let me trust you. That's all we have: trust in each other. If you feel like it's too much, you let me know up here, and we'll have no hard feelings. Down there, if I feel like I can't trust you, if I think that you're putting the team in danger, I'll kill you myself."

Tim actually smiled at the threat upon his life. He knew that it really wasn't personal. "Yes, sir."

Orpheus turned sideways just enough to offer his hand. "Welcome to Scalpel."

Tim accepted the offered hand and gave what he hoped was a firm pump. Orpheus didn't seem to be the type who'd be impressed by such things, but it couldn't hurt. "Thank you."

"One mission from now you won't be thanking

me. Now, did Sam give you something for me?"

Tim panicked for a moment when he couldn't find the tubes right away, but they were safe in his cargo pocket. *Whew.* He handed the tubes over.

Orpheus uncapped one and slid out a cigar. Tim thought that this might have been his cue to leave, but he hadn't been dismissed, either. He had no idea what to do.

"You smoke cigars, Tim?"

"Umm, never have."

"Well you do now." With that, he slid out the second cigar, clipped them both, and handed one to Tim, who awkwardly put it in his mouth. Orpheus produced a lighter, lit his slowly and methodically, then handed the lighter to Tim. The novice mimicked the older man well enough to get his lit. The smoke tasted bitter at first, and he inhaled a little, but he fought back the urge to cough. The next few pulls were smoother, and he thought he could get used to it.

They spent the next forty minutes or so on the rooftop, overlooking the city, the silence only occasionally broken by a question from Tim. Orpheus was very patient and he answered every inquiry, if curtly.

When they were both down to nubs, Orpheus told Tim to get some sleep. As he got to the stairwell door, Tim said, "Sir, I have one more question."

"Go ahead."

"The reason you do this...does it have something to do with your name?"

"It's just a nickname that Fish gave me, Tim. Nothing more than that."

"I know a bit of mythology, and Orpheus was the

guy who went into the underworld to rescue his wife. It didn't turn out well."

The man known as Orpheus showed Tim his back, dropped his cigar to the roof and ground it beneath a booted toe.

New Twist on an Old Mission

"This is it? This is the whole team?"

"What were you expecting, Bait?"

Tim didn't know what he was expecting, except that he figured there would be more of the team. "Five of us? I just guessed that the team would be bigger, that's all."

Fish chuckled. "Doing what we do as a big team would get us all killed."

"Truth," Mutt agreed.

Orpheus entered the locker room and said, "Gentlemen."

"Hey, Bossman, just in time. Bait here was questioning your decision to keep the team as small as it is. He thinks we should be a battalion."

An increasing look of horror dawned on Bait's face. "I did not! Uh, sir. I just, I..."

"Relax. He's playing with you," Sam said.

Tim forced a laugh and muttered, "Fucker" in Fish's direction. He slung his AR15 (liberated from a local gun store during Scalpel's first mission) over his head so that the sling ran diagonally across his chest.

"Oh, boy, don't do that," Mutt warned.

"Why? What did I do?"

His answer came in the form of Orpheus wrapping his hand around the rifle and yanking him back forcefully. He moved his face closer and showed his teeth. "Now, imagine me chewing your face off."

"Okay! I get it!"

The rest of the men in the room were trying to stifle their laughter when Orpheus snarled, "And the rest of you...maybe I missed the part where this all became a fucking joke to you, when we decided that looking out for each other should take a back seat to laughing because the new guy's doing it wrong. So help him out." He looked around the room, pausing on each face. "You want another one on your conscience?"

There were a few mumbles in response.

"What was that?"

"No, sir," was the next response, and it came in much clearer this time.

"Good. Because if I'd taken the same approach in the beginning, you'd-" He was interrupted by a chirping noise coming from his hip. He unclipped the walkie and said, "Holt."

A female voice responded, "Hey, Cam. Trager wants to see you."

Orpheus sighed. "He does realize that we're ten minutes away from an insertion, right?"

"Yep. He says it's important."

"Of course it is. Thanks, Lena."

"Welcome. Out."

He pointed at Mutt. "Remind me to finish my point when we're not hip deep in dead people." He didn't wait for Mutt to say anything before he walked out.

Mutt laughed and said to the door, "Yeah, I'll do

that, boss."

Fish said, "Wow, he might have been a little perturbed."

"He's right, though."

"Yeah, yeah."

Tim, who had remained silent since Orpheus had finished his quick lesson asked, "What did he mean? When he said 'another one on your conscience'?"

Fish said, "Let me field this one." He out an arm around Bait's shoulders and said in a surprisingly warm and conversational tone. "Ever see the movie Spinal Tap?"

Bait thought for a second. "That fake documentary? Bits and pieces, why?"

"Well, a running theme throughout the movie was their drummer. See, the band couldn't keep one; they kept dying in weird ways. I remember that one guy choked to death on someone else's vomit. Another died while he was gardening. One actually exploded on stage! It was freakin' hilarious."

Bait just looked at him for a second when he got the point. "I'm the newest drummer, right?"

"Yup."

"How many before me?"

Fish made a show of counting on his fingers. Tim started worrying when it went to a second hand. "You'll be the fourth."

"What happened to the other ones?"

"All sorts of weird shit. The second one that we had freaked out when he saw a few Sprinters and ran off the first floor of a building that was under construction. Normally, not that bad a decision, except he landed on exposed rebar. That was not pretty. Another guy got eaten by his own uncle when he strayed too far from the rest of us. His uncle was a Jekyll, and the idiot got too close. Tore his throat out by the time I got there and put them both down."

"What's a Jekyll?"

Mutt stood up. "During your training, we showed you the two common kinds of zombie: Sprinters and Shufflers. There's no difference between them but time or exertion, really. If a zombie is relatively fresh..."

"That's exactly why we should call them Freshmen and not Sprinters! 'Fresh men!' Get it?"

"Shut it, Fish. If a zombie is new, recently turned, those bastards can move as fast as they ever could. However, their muscles can't regenerate, so as they exert themselves and deteriorate because they're, uh, dead, they get torn down pretty quickly. They become Shufflers." Fish opened his mouth but Mutt cut him off. "Shut it, Fish."

Tim nodded. "The slow ones."

"Yes."

"And the Jekyll?"

"That's the third type, and it's the one we can't prepare you for. You can either handle it or you can't."

"You're not even going to tell me?"

"Bait, you probably won't have to wait long to see it with your own eyes."

Tim switched gears. "I don't suppose you'll stop calling me that."

"What? Bait? Not happening right now, because until you prove otherwise, that's probably be what you're best at." Fish adopted the same conversational tone he'd exhibited earlier. "Tell you what, though. Live long enough, prove yourself, and I will personally give you a real nickname."

* * *

Orpheus sat in the chair on the subordinate side of the large mahogany desk and couldn't believe what he was just told. "Say that again?"

Martin Trager, CEO of Lost Whaler General, repeated himself. "You need to capture, not kill, a Jekyll and return it here. More than one, if possible."

"You're joking. I've lost more men to Jekylls than the other two combined!"

"I know, I know, but hear me out." He said nothing for a few seconds while he fiddled with some papers. "We think there might be a cure."

Orpheus snickered. "Yeah, a cure for dead. Sure."

"Don't be an ass," Trager snapped. "Those people are gone, naturally. They need to be exterminated before we can start over here. And we will start over. This is my island, and I intend to hang on to it."

"Can we get on with it, Marty? My team's waiting on me."

"As I was saying, Dr. Vincent believes that there is a cure. Maybe 'cure' is the wrong word. Let's go with 'inoculation' instead. History has shown us that plagues of all kinds eventually come back. We thought we wiped out polio, but isolated cases are starting to pop up again. And in the case of this infection, an isolated case is all that might be needed to start a full-blown outbreak again."

Orpheus stood up and rested his hands on the desk. He leaned forward, all controlled aggression. "Where does a Jekyll figure in?"

Trager mimicked the stance, giving the standoff a physical manifestation. "You've seen them. They're somewhere between life and unlife. My researchers think that those poor saps contain something inside of them that fights off the infection, if only in short bursts. They'll eventually die and change, but their makeup makes the process last a whole lot longer. If we can isolate it and synthesize it, we can maybe avoid this same kind of horror in the future."

Orpheus rubbed his palms together while he thought about it.

"You can say, 'Sure, Mr. Trager' anytime now."

"Hold on, I'm still figuring out your angle."

Trager didn't like the delay, or the implication. "If I've given you the impression that this is a request, I apologize. Get me some Jekylls, or your little field trips are over. That's a promise."

"And all the survivors?"

"You mean if there still are any? Collateral damage, I'm afraid."

Orpheus fought the urge to slap the other man in his head, and said, "Fine. We go in, grab one, and extract like normal, but I get to go back in before the reap if I think I've missed anything."

"Done." Trager sat down, satisfied.

Orpheus turned around when he got to the door. "Threaten to take your resources away from me again, after all I've been through, and I'll fuck you up."

"Feel free to slam the door behind you on your way out." Orpheus left it wide open, and Trager was glad to see him go.

* * *

"You've gotta be kiddin' me," Mutt said.

"Yeah, that's what I said. But they think they might be able to pull some good out of it, so we have to try. We've come up dry on the last two runs, anyway."

"Don't remind me. Do you think there are any more survivors on the island?"

Orpheus wrestled with whether or not to lie to his new best friend. He decided against it. "Honestly, no, but I have to know for sure. I'm not in this for much more, but I'm in for that, at least. After that, well...yeah."

"Yeah."

"Where's the team?"

"On the pad, waiting for us."

The First Run

Tim wondered if the sweating would ever go away. Then he wondered if he ever wanted it to. He was on edge and as alert as he'd ever been. The roar of the helicopter rotors barely registered as he checked, double-checked, and triple-checked his gear. He watched the others, and it was obvious that they'd worked together for a long time and had their routines down. Up near the pilot, Orpheus and Mutt handed their gear back and forth to be checked by the other man. Fish and Sam did the same in their seats opposite of

118

Tim's.

So where's my buddy? he thought as he checked his gear for a fourth time. Sam seemed to read his thoughts, or his expression, and started checking Tim's gear. Tim was thankful, and tried to say as much over the cacophony.

He patted Sam on the shoulder and yelled, "Thanks!" Sam responded with a thumbs-up and continued. He tightened up a few straps on the jumpsuit and was finished. He settled back into his seat and closed his eyes. Meditation, prayer, or both. Tim wished that he was relaxed enough to be able to do that.

Instead, he looked over his shoulder at Orpheus. He cradled something in his hands, and Tim could make out that it was another pistol, only smaller than his primary. He figured it for a backup, probably strapped into an ankle holster. He wasn't sure if anyone else had one, only that he sure didn't. Maybe he'd ask Orpheus about it when they got back to the tower.

Not for the first time, Tim wondered why in God's name they had to do this at night.

* * *

Tim asked Mutt why they didn't insert during daylight hours.

"We go in at night. That may seem counter-intuitive, but it gives us the best chance of moving around unnoticed. These things possess the same tools that living humans have, and for a lot longer than you'd think. If they have eyes, they can see. If they have ears, they can hear. At night, we take their vision out of the equation while we still have it, thanks to technology."

119

He motioned towards the night vision rig.

"The night vision is nice but, like all technology, there is a chance it will fail you when you most need it. It's supplemental, that's all. And don't think that a zombie with no eyes, ears, or nose can't find you, because they can. We have no idea how it works, but they can find a living person like a damn homing pigeon finds its roost. Your most valuable tools are located on either side of your head. Your second most valuable is right in the middle of your face. Pay attention to them. You'll live a lot longer."

* * *

The helicopter hovered ten feet above the roof of the library in downtown. Fish yelled, "On my heels, Bait!" and jumped without another word. He flexed his knees and rolled into it, popping up gracefully into a crouch with his pistol raised. Tim hesitated only briefly before he followed suit. The impact from that height was unexpected, but he rolled with it and came up in the same position.

"Not bad!"

Tim nodded and tried to ignore the throbbing in his knee as he watched the remaining three men exit, Orpheus last. The copilot dropped several black bags and flashed a thumbs-up. Orpheus returned it and the copilot disappeared behind the tinted glass. Ten seconds later, the helicopter was gaining altitude and heading back to the hospital.

After the helicopter was mostly out of earshot, Orpheus said, "Let's move."

"Why?" Tim asked. To him, the library roof

seemed like a good place to set up.

Mutt replied, "If you're thinking that this is a nice spot to camp and make s'mores, you're right. Unfortunately, we just made a highly-visible entrance and a helluva racket. We don't know what might be coming for us. So we move and wait." He pointed over Tim's shoulder. "Right there."

Tim looked and saw that he was pointing to the building next door. Tim had grown up on the island, and, though he'd never seen it from this angle, he knew that they were next to the old movie theater, The Classic. Tim grabbed a bag without being told and walked to the edge. It wasn't a terrible jump, only about eight feet, but being three stories up made it seem like twenty. It seemed like fifty when Tim saw some shadows moving in the alley beneath him. The shadows seemed to be moving in the same general direction, and that direction was right at them.

Something made a loud pounding noise behind them, and they all whirled with their pistols up. They heard it again and realized that something was repeatedly slamming against the door to the roof. Suddenly, Tim agreed wholeheartedly with the decision to move next door. Orpheus motioned for Mutt to take Fish and Tim with him to the next roof. They threw the bags over the gap. Fish backed up a few paces then rocketed forward, pushing off the ledge and clearing the gap by a mile. He got up and mimed a little air guitar before he began slowly searching the roof. Tim caught Mutt rolling his eyes a bit and then he followed Fish. The rookie brought up the rear and made the jump with surprising ease. His two companions seemed a little surprised that he didn't come up way short and end up dangling from the ledge.

The three of them did a quick sweep of the roof. It was empty, so they took up positions and got as low as they could while still being able to see Orpheus and Sam. The boss motioned for Sam to make the jump while he kept his pistol trained on the door. Tim expected Orpheus to be right behind, but he paused on the roof. He walked back towards the door and grabbed the handle. He started to push the latch down with his thumb, and Tim looked at Mutt with a panicked look.

Mutt's face showed nothing.

"What is he doing?" Tim whispered.

"Don't know. Stay ready." To emphasize his point, he pulled a spare magazine and laid it next to him. Sam hustled to the pile of bags and opened one. He pulled out a shotgun and took up a position next to Mutt.

Fish had his back to the rest, guarding their backsides.

Tim resisted the urge to wrap his finger around the trigger. He was tense enough that accidentally firing it was a definite possibility.

Orpheus hadn't moved in a few seconds. He turned his head to look at something past the door and appeared frozen. Tim realized that Orpheus wasn't looking at something; he was listening for something.

After a few more seconds, Orpheus let the handle return to its original position slowly. He backed away from the door, holstered his sidearm, and made the jump.

"What in the hell was that?"

"Let's set up, Sam. Then we can talk."

* * *

Orpheus finished telling the others about the new wrinkle while they set up their gear. The roof of the movie theater was meant to serve as their "command post." In practice, it meant this was where they'd store the gear they couldn't carry, and where they'd come to rest until they were ready to extract.

Fish was the first to speak after Orpheus finished. "Sooooo...we're supposed to grab a snarling, spitting, screaming Jekyll, bag or whatever the Hell else we can do to subdue it...and get it back here for pickup while trying to not alert the zombies that we already have a hard enough time avoiding when it's just us."

Orpheus laughed. "That's about right."

"Well, I must say, I'm psyched. When can we get started?"

"Let's eat. Then we have to head over to the reap zone for the walkies. Tim, that bag has the MREs in it." Orpheus sat down on an exhaust fan housing and rubbed his neck. The rest of the men got as comfortable as they could while Tim rummaged through the bag. He pulled out an MRE, squinted to read it in the moonlight, and said, "Uh, who wants hot dogs?"

Sam said, "Just throw us whatever."

"Oh, okay." Tim tossed a package to each man, but kept the hot dogs for himself. They ate mostly in silence, and Tim was surprised at how peaceful everything seemed. If he didn't know any better, they were just five guys on a camping trip. On the roof of a movie theater. Surrounded by the walking dead.

"Trager had a point, as much as I'm loathe to admit it," Orpheus said. "If we survive...by 'we' I mean

123

'mankind'...we have to believe that the outbreak could happen again. If we find a Jekyll, and a cure comes from that, then we did some good work."

Mutt said, "We've already done good work, O. A shitload of it. You especially."

"We're talking about the future, though. We owe it to the survivors, don't we?"

"Yeah, Sam, we do. I get what we're doing here; I just don't like having it sprung on us with no warning at all. That's a pretty big curveball to throw at us."

"Maybe we'll end up in the history books," Tim offered. "That would be something, wouldn't it?"

"You know what else would be something? Being around to read it." Mutt consolidated his trash and placed it back into the bag. "Eh, no sense wasting daylight, so to speak. We ready?"

"Lead the way, brutha," Fish said. He clapped his hands. "Let's go grab ourselves a psycho."

"I don't think that we'll have to look hard," Orpheus said, and Tim immediately figured out what he meant.

"That's what you were listening for over there. You think that you heard a Jekyll, whatever that is."

"Mmm. Here's what we do. Clear the theater, head over to the dead zone next door, pick up the walkies and whatever else we can find, drop the walkies into this zone, come back up, and pull that thing right through that door. If I'm right, and I think that I am, we can grab and extract within a few minutes."

Several heads nodded at this. Tim saw the deep respect and blind trust that they all had in Orpheus. He could see how that would happen. His confidence was very soothing, considering their surroundings. Tim wondered how much of it was bravado intended to keep his team's morale up.

"Any questions?"

Tim raised his hand.

"This isn't geometry class. What do you need?"

Tim put his hand down and felt like an idiot when he asked, "Would someone please tell me what a Jekyll is?"

Back on the Ranch

Selena Moore knew that Trager would not be happy with what she was doing right now. His only concern was getting what he wanted: money, top-shelf booze, women, and, of course, power. He hid it surprisingly well beneath a facade of manners and cultivated humility, even a maddening charm that worked on Lena more than she was comfortable admitting. Once you saw him for what he was, a selfish prick who would use anyone to get what he wanted and then discard them, you felt better.

What he wanted right now was a Jekyll, and he was using Orpheus to do it.

Lena didn't like that. Not one bit.

All Orpheus wanted to do was finish his business and be left alone. He'd already given far more to the island and whoever was left than anyone else could have imagined. Still, he had unfinished business, and Trager knew it. He leveraged Orpheus' personal mission into one that would, Lena had no doubt, benefit him and only him in the end.

125

She wanted to know what his angle was, but she had come up empty so far.

A crackling noise came from the bank of radios set up against the far wall. She quickly rolled her chair back with a thrust of her legs and figured out that it was coming from the shortwave. She opened her own mic and said, "Caller, if you can hear me, repeat last transmission." She didn't expect to get a response; she was fairly certain that she'd heard nothing more significant than random static. But she had to try.

"Caller, repeat last."

Nothing.

She hung the mic back on its hook and rolled back to her desk. She closed the book for the time being on what she called "Project: Snake" in her head. There were two hidden files on her computer: that one and "Project: Lost Soul." She opened this file and started poring over everything she had learned about the lone open file: Ethan Holt.

Where could he be?

Twenty minutes went by before another radio transmission came through. This one was crystal clear, and expected. "Lena, it's Sam."

Lena keyed her mic, mindful that this frequency was monitored by Trager's goon squad. For some reason, they didn't think that anyone else knew about it, but they only had Lena fooled for about ten seconds. "Go, Sam."

"We're initiating retrieval of the walkies, and then we'll begin the sweep of the theater and surrounding buildings before we work our way back up to the roof for extraction. Hope to have a Jekyll in tow. If everything goes well, we'll be silent for a few hours, at least."

"And if it doesn't go well?"

"Then we'll be silent a lot longer."

"That's funny. How's the rookie look?"

"Too early to tell, but he seems to have some balls. That's something."

"Okay. Take care of them."

She heard Fish yell off-mic but clear, "His balls?" Lena shook her head and chuckled.

"Shut it, Fish. Will do. Oh, and don't tell those Scythe boys this, but I find them all very sexually arousing. Out."

Lena held back her laughter long enough to croak, "Out." She giggled for a few moments more and then got to work. She went to the large plastic-covered map of the island, found the area that the Scalpel team was going to search, and wrote "2140" in grease pencil over the theater. Tracking their progress was her favorite part of being the dispatcher/resident techie for the team. She liked to imagine that she was right there with them, doing some dirty work.

In reality, all she really did was answer the radio, chart their movements, and then send in those death-dealers to "sanitize" the areas. She knew why Orpheus and his team didn't let up at all during their searches. They knew that, as soon as they were extracted, everything living and unliving alike would be wiped off the face of the planet, and Orpheus' past failures and desire to not let any innocents die drove him to the edge time and again. His team was the same way: they all had demons. But, unlike a lot of people, they used those demons to push themselves farther.

They saved lives. And they could very well be

instrumental in the survival of the human species.

She could at least help them, and him, in any way she possibly could.

＊ ＊ ＊

Trager swiped his ID card and entered the outer viewing ring of the laboratory. He was still amazed at the design of this building, even though he'd all but personally swung every visible and back-alley deal to make it happen; it was put together with such forethought that it was easy to forget the world that existed just outside the doors to the street.

It had been fairly easy to convert most of the rooms into living quarters. There was no shortage of beds, even with the patients that had been there when the crisis had kicked off. Many of them had died as, unfortunately, they just didn't have enough people to keep up the excellent standard of care he prided himself on. They had running water, heat, and electricity courtesy of the solar panels and wind turbines mounted in strategic places on the exterior of the building. They had a massive store of food thanks to the efforts of the retrieval crews, and they'd even put together an impressive garden on the observation decks.

They had, in short order, converted this marvel of a building into a thriving mini-city.

Trager intended to continue making lemons into lemonade.

He walked slowly around the lab which was viewable from all angles courtesy of the wall of plexiglass that defined the interior research space. Several people were busy inside, either hunched over computer terminals, chemicals, or the dozens of thrashing undead that Anders had managed to procure. Locked inside one of those things was the answer.

That was the thinking, anyway.

The zombie virus or whatever the Hell it was was proving to be a slippery little devil. They couldn't pin it down enough to the point where they could analyze it to the fullest and gather the information that they needed. They kept at it, but every attempt at a cure had failed. The most intelligent minds in the city were all stumped.

Trager rapped on the glass and gestured to one of the researchers. The researcher consulted a few instruments before waving Trager in. He swiped his card again and a door slid open with a faint hiss.

"How are we, Vin?" he asked of the researcher.

"Not good. I can tell you everything about how the virus acts around dead flesh, but I don't have a clue how it attacks and corrupts living people. We need a fresher subject."

"I've already made arrangements. You should have one within the next day or two." He looked around the room at the captive zombies. "Can you learn anything else from them? If not, we should throw them out."

Vin said, "Maybe. Maybe not. I'd like to keep them around for a little while longer, if I can. A few are so decomposed that they're just taking up space, though."

"I'll leave it up to you, but let's not keep them any longer than we have to. I knew a couple of these people. They were assholes in life, but..."

"Of course."

Trager walked to the door and swiped his card. When it opened, he turned around and said, "I'm going through a lot of trouble to give you what you're requesting, Vin. Once I do, I expect results." He saw in the other man's face that his point, and meaning, had been taken as intended. Satisfied, he opened the stairwell and headed to the fifth floor to check on the mission's progress.

The Theater

They cleared the theater from the top down. Nobody was in the hallways. They moved silently, in sync with each other to the point that they rarely even needed to use hand signals, let alone speak.

All except for Tim. For his part, he stayed close to Orpheus, as he'd been ordered to do.

The door to the projector room was closed. Orpheus signaled for their newest member to show what he'd learned so far. Tim nodded and went to the door, put his ear to the gap between the door and the frame, and stood absolutely motionless, listening. When he was certain that, at the very least, nothing was moving in there, he opened the door as quietly as possible.

I should be more nervous than this, he thought. This is real, not training. Then again, I didn't have anyone watching my back then, either. He took a snapshot of each man's location and then, slightly emboldened, opened the door in one slow, smooth motion. Orpheus helped him out by shining his red lens

LED flashlight into the room ahead of him. The red light saved their natural night vision, but the glow it cast was almost creepy enough to make Tim wish for a million or more candlepower spotlight.

Orpheus entered the room just behind and swept the beam from left to right quickly then back again. Tim saw a dark shape slumped over a desk right next to the projector. He knew right away that it was a person; his only question was whether or not the person was dead or something worse. He moved forward to find out for sure but stopped short of touching the body. He could see that something was wrapped tightly around the dead man's neck. A closer inspection revealed that it was a belt.

Suicide. That's better than the alternative. That could just as easily have been me. He wanted to confirm his diagnosis, so he put his hand on the dead man's shoulder and turned him over enough to do a cursory check of the body. There were no obvious bite marks.

You died as yourself. Good one on you, pal.

He gave Orpheus a thumbs up and walked over to the small window next to the projector. He looked below into the seating area but couldn't make out a thing. He pulled out a compact set of night vision goggles and switched them on. The room below was immediately bathed in a green glow...

Red light, green light, it's like Christmas...

...and he started counting zombies.

He counted twice and got eight both times. He flashed five fingers then three more to let Orpheus know the count.

Orpheus said, "We're safe to talk right now.

131

Hand them over." He held out his hand to receive the goggles. He looked through them for a few seconds and said, "Training opportunity. Let's say I wanted you to go down there and put them down. How would you do it?"

Tim wasn't sure if it was a test or a trick question or some other kind of setup, so he decided to just answer the question honestly and hoped that Orpheus approved. "I wouldn't. First thing I'd do would be look for a way to avoid them. Barring that, I'd slide open that window and shoot them from up here."

"Not bad. But this one time, we're going to take them head on. You need to bust your cherry in a semi-controlled environment before you step in some real shit. Understand?"

"Yes, sir."

"Lead the way."

Tim took point and motioned for the others to follow him. When they got to the entrance to the theater Tim was about to request some light when two high-powered beams flared behind him. His own shadow startled him for a second, but he thought that went unnoticed. He hoped so.

Orpheus and Mutt were the two who weren't holding flashlights, and they had their weapons raised and ready. Mutt put his free hand on the door and said, "Don't freak. You got backup," and opened the door much faster than Tim would have liked.

Tim dropped the first one with a clean shot to the head before any of them had turned around.

After that, things got a little tense.

* * *

132

When the first one dropped, Tim thought it might be a piece of cake. When he dropped the second, thought he may have given the zombies too much credit to rise to the level of piece of cake. They were slow, and too uncoordinated to even figure out a way to get to him because of the obstacles that the rows of seats presented.

To punish him for being cocky, a Sprinter who had been shambling only seconds before started down the aisle at him. A second one actually began climbing clumsily, but effectively, over the seats.

I had no idea they could do that.

Rationally, Tim knew that the zombies, regardless of how old or new, lacked the higher brain functions involved in deceit. They simply reacted to the new stimulus.

However, his paranoid mind believed that the bastards had been playing possum.

Thankfully, his body reacted faster than his mind did, and he took the Sprinter in the aisle with two shots to the chest. It wasn't dead, but it did get tangled up under the seats when it fell, and Tim felt extremely lucky for that as the second one vaulted over the last two rows separating the two of them.

Only one thought flashed through Tim's mind as the airborne zombie closed in on him: *I don't have time to shoot.* He instinctively thrust his hands forward, dropped his weapon in the process, and used the zombie's momentum to propel it safely past into the seats several rows away. Tim heard something crunch when it landed, but he was under no illusions that whatever had broken in its body would stop it from coming again.

Tim scrambled for his gun and knocked it further under the seats. He looked over his shoulder and, as he'd feared, the zombie had righted itself and was coming towards him again, its arm bent at a weird angle at the elbow.

Tim heard a pop and the Sprinter dropped where it stood. A few more followed and the rest of the zombies, most of which Tim had forgotten about while he dealt with the immediate threats, followed suit. In the span of a few seconds the theater had gone from out of control to completely silent, the faint wisps of gunsmoke providing the only movement. Tim felt his chest rising and falling with rapid, nearly panicked breaths, and he had to work to slow them down to normal.

Everything that had been dead once was dead again, this time for good.

Tim looked at Orpheus, who was replacing the rounds in his magazine. "Not bad. Grab your weapon and let's move." That was all he said; he and Mutt started laughing about something while they searched the bodies. Tim found his pistol and replaced his own rounds, as well.

Sam said, "Nice move. Don't ever drop your weapon, though. We may not always be around to have your back."

Tim nodded.

"Search time, bait," Fish said. "Quick and dirty."

They all started going through pockets and purses.

"What am I supposed to be looking for?"

"Anything useful. Food, medications, cameras, and cell phones with cameras. Grab every one of those.

134

Memory cards will do, too."

"Why those?"

"Boss's orders," Sam said, looking in Orpheus' direction.

"Good enough." They spent the next five minutes grabbing what they could. Tim's final tally: 2 cell phones, a digital camera, a keychain multi-tool, a can of pepper spray, three packs of gum, a roll of breath mints, and a condom.

"Nice haul," Fish teased. "C'mon bait, time to play pack mule. Turn around." Tim did so and Fish unzipped the compartment that had been sewn into the back of his jumpsuit. "Everybody, load up." When they were done,Tim was lugging an extra five pounds, and Fish was passing out gum.

They formed up, Tim right in the middle, next to Orpheus, who asked, "How do you feel?"

"I'm okay. A little freaked out, but okay."

"Good. I had to know if you could handle the real thing."

"And?"

Orpheus deadpanned. "You're still here."

"The worst part was how quiet they were. They didn't make a sound."

"Everyone says the same thing the first time. I know I did. I expected moaning and screaming and shit like that, too. But they're dead, bait." Fish playfully poked Tim in the forehead. "They got no air in their lungs."

Tim mentally slapped himself for missing something so obvious.

"That was a pretty sweet move you pulled, except I would've shot that fucker in the air like skeet."

135

"I bet you would have, Fish. I guess I was too busy trying not to shit myself."

* * *

Their chosen landing site was no accident; it was one of the few places on the island that could accommodate a landing and takeoff, and it was as close to an inert "reap zone" that they could get. They stayed in the shadows as much as possible, scouting each area with the night vision before they continued. They moved at a plodding pace, but it was a lot better than rushing into something that they couldn't rush out of. Along the way, Tim watched his mates as much as he watched his surroundings. He emulated their movements, and he tried to learn to read their body language to lessen the need for speech or even hand signals.

In this place, the quieter, the better.

The silence was almost absolute, save for the occasional flutter of bat wings or chirping of an insect. Those were the times when Tim relaxed a little bit, because he knew that where zombies were, animals weren't, and vice versa. When the silence descended again, so did the tension. If the other four felt the same way, they didn't show it, so Tim tried not to, either.

They must have sneaked by dozens of zombies (and hundreds of corpses), almost without incident. There was a moment when they came upon a bottleneck of cars that almost completely blocked the street. Zombies were plugging the only two gaps large enough to accommodate a human, but Mutt resorted to the old "throw a bottle and watch them chase the noise" trick to move them.

After that, there was smooth sailing to the courthouse. The closer they got to the reap zone, the more the zombie population thinned out, until finally there were none. They made it to the courthouse. Orpheus decided against entering through the front door and instead led the team down the alley to the right of it. He knew the door was locked, because he was the one who had locked it a few weeks previous. He also had the key, and he used it. He held the rest of his team back as a rush of stale air came out to greet him. He sniffed the air and made a face of disgust. A few seconds later the smell hit Tim, and he assumed he made a similar face. It smelled awful, like rotting produce.

"We're good," Orpheus said, and he swung the door wider. He turned on his flashlight and entered, not all that cautiously, Tim noticed.

* * *

Once they were inside, they took a breather. They found some comfortable chairs in the waiting room and plopped down into them. Fish decided to take a power nap (how anyone could sleep under the circumstances was beyond Tim) while the other four munched on some energy bars. Between mouthfuls Orpheus said, "Once we clear as many buildings as we can before 0400 hours or so, we drop a few walkies here and there. We leave, close up so no strays can get in, and get back to the extraction point. We broadcast a message on the walkies telling people where to meet us or where we can find them, and that they only have a few hours before we leave. That's when Lena sends in

Scythe."

Tim had an idea what Scythe was for, but he was still very interested.

"Scythe is a necessary evil. We have to retake this town if we're to have any hope whatsoever of keeping the human race alive. If...if...we can do that, we stand an okay chance of surviving and bouncing all the way back. We are on an island, after all. If whatever started all of this is wiped out along with all of the zombies, we might make it."

Orpheus took another bite and continued. "They pump the buildings we cleared with a persistent chemical agent that eats any organic matter it comes in contact with. Seeing as they pump it anywhere and everywhere, including blowing it through the ventilation shafts, that means that all organic matter it comes in contact with disappears in under a week. Even bones. Any zombies we skip over...or flat-out miss...go away."

"And any living people we miss, too," Tim added. He was starting to understand what he'd signed up for, and he felt a small sense of pride in his decision.

"Exactly. That's why what we do is so important. Anything less than perfection means that someone who needs our help, who needs saving, dies. None too pleasantly, either."

Another bite. "I've had enough of death. We all have."

"I get it, sir."

"You need to understand one thing, Tim: once Scythe comes in, they do not stop for any reason. They are a fail-safe. They're single-minded when it comes to their reaping: they will do it. They're not combat troops, but what they have in spades is a complete lack of empathy for other human beings."

Sam said, "It's true. We tried to call them off once because we thought we got a transmission on the walkie. Lena tried to buy us thirty minutes to check it out and be sure, but they went about their business. If we'd been in their way, I don't think they would have thought twice about greasing us. They might have enjoyed it even more, I don't know."

"Who are they?"

"Survivors like us," Orpheus continued. "This team right here, there's a reason we stick together, a reason why any one of us would die to protect the others. Scythe, on the other hand, is made up of, for lack of a better word, sociopaths. They enjoy killing just a little too much."

"That seems like a dangerous group to give weapons to."

"It is. But they're perfectly suited to walking into this place and mowing down every zombie they see. I think I knew that when I inadvertently founded them."

* * *

Holt disappeared into the bowels of the building for a while, as Mutt knew he would, because he did it every mission. "His 'me' time," he explained to Tim. "So leave him alone. In the meantime, I'll tell you a story."

Scythe began when Cameron Holt was blinded by anger, and he'd found a group of like-minded men to join him. They went among the survivors that were housed in the hospital and found whatever weapons they could, which wasn't much. One of the men, Anders was his name, had the idea to raid the weapons cache of the private firm that provided the building security. They disarmed a guard and forced him to open the weapons safe ("Almost puked with a gun in my face," Fish added). Holt even went so far as to threaten his life if he didn't comply. He was never quite sure if he really meant it or not, but months later he was still afraid that he might have.

Weapons in hand, Holt had no greater plan than to go out into the streets and kill as many of the creatures that had taken his family from him as he could before he ended up dead. His rage emboldened the other men, and they took to the battle.

Holt stood on the street and looked for a target. Their immediate area was clear. The remains of the small island police force had barricaded both sides of the street and were engaging a large mob of the undead. This sight focused him a little; he looked through the windows of the hospital building at the panicked mass of people inside. He knew that he could do something more productive than just random zombie-killing. He was, for the moment, capable of trying to protect the people behind him. Holt and half of his impromptu army joined one barricade; Anders and the rest joined the other.

There were only two officers left in Holt's barricade. He took up position right next to the one with the most stripes on his arm, picked out a target, and fired. The zombie fell and made the large pile of dead-again bodies slightly bigger. That pile was dwarfed by the amount of zombies still on their feet. There were easily hundreds, and their numbers seemed to be growing by the minute.

He chose another target and fired.

The sergeant yelled without turning his head. "Normally, I'd tell you to get the fuck inside and let us handle it, but we need all the help we can get!"

"Is this it? Is this what you have left?"

"Most of my guys are with them now!" Holt didn't have to see the sergeant's nod toward the undead to know what he meant. "All comm's down. No cells, land lines, we even have a satellite phone that shit the bed! We're on our own, pal!"

Holt chose another target and took it down. His approach was almost robotic: point, shoot, point, shoot. Reload. Point, shoot. He tried to block out the worrisome whoops and cheers from the other men he'd "recruited" and just think about the next target, especially the fast ones. But all he could really think about was the island's population: approximately 30,000. And that didn't count the summer folk that probably pushed the number closer to forty.

The dozen of them had no chance of holding them off.

None.

"Sarge, we gotta get inside!"

"I-we-" The sergeant was torn between his duty and the painful truth. "Fuck it, live to fight another day, I hope! Fall back into the building doubletime!" Holt echoed it as loud as he could, but the other group either didn't hear him or ignored it altogether. "Anders, you idiot, pull them back!"

Anders definitely heard that. He turned around and smiled. Holt knew right away that he'd made a mistake in throwing in with that man in any capacity at all. If he was ever all there, he wasn't anymore, and Holt knew that he would have to deal with him at some point.

For now, he began to move toward the building, and Holt found himself being slightly disappointed that the time wouldn't be now. They retreated to the stairwell and started to file to the first floor.

The rest happened fast, but it seemed to take forever.

A blue box truck careened through the mob, knocking bodies flying. It clipped one of the police cars as it tried to sneak by and was knocked into a sideways slide. Its wheels hit the sidewalk and it overturned. Its momentum carried it halfway into the parking area under the building before it came to a stop. The mob changed course and headed for the truck.

The cargo doors were pushed open, and four people fell out. They were shaken up but fought to their feet as the zombies closed in. They screamed for help.

The sergeant yelled, "Cover 'em, for Christ's sake!"

They fired behind the four people as carefully as they could, but soon they threw caution to the wind. Holt thought there was a lot of them before, at the blockade. When both of them were overrun and the two separate groups joined together, he realized how dire their situation really was. The only positive thing was that the throng of zombies was so tightly packed that the men would have to actually try to miss with their bullets.

Not that any of it was doing the survivors from the truck much good. Two of them were pulled backwards and swallowed by the mob no more than forty feet from the truck. The third fell only fifteen feet or so after that.

Holt yelled encouragement to the fourth who hobbled as quickly as he could on what appeared to be a broken ankle. "Come on! You're almost there!" He tried to believe his own words, because the zombies were closing the gap between themselves and the survivor faster than he was between himself and relative safety.

A fast zombie broke from the pack and Holt immediately targeted him as the most immediate threat. He hit the thing twice, but its momentum carried it forward where it crashed into the survivor and they tumbled to the ground. He screamed, "Get it off! GET IT OFF!" as he fought to keep its jaws away from his throat. *He's not gonna make it*, Holt thought. *Goddammit*. The survivor managed to throw off the lone zombie, but the rest had caught up and were starting to tear at his clothes and flesh. Holt had had enough and emptied his magazine into the poor bastard. It was the very least he could do, and he promised himself that he would be better the next time.

The five of them...Holt, the sergeant, Anders, and the two remaining members of their impromptu assault force...took the stairs three at a time as the door slammed shut behind them. The heavy metal door and the thick concrete that surrounded them served to insulate them from the insanity outside, if only temporarily.

That came to an end as soon as they opened the door to the first floor. The scene outside was awful; inside was almost worse. Here was a study in what hundreds upon hundreds of terrified people could do to each other when in a confined space. It was a combination of employees, people from the outside seeking sanctuary, and patients seeking information. There was screaming, crying, threats, fist fights, and impotent orders from the thoroughly overmatched security personnel. The din inside made Holt realize how quiet their recent battle with the undead had really been.

He felt a tap on his shoulder. "Hey, thanks for your help out there, uh..." the sergeant stammered.

"Cameron Holt."

The sergeant nodded a hello. "Randolph Mutters. Mutt, to people I've fought beside. Hey, Holt, can I count on you here?"

"Of course. Do your thing."

He blew a protracted breath between clenched teeth, not looking forward to calming the scene in front of him. He climbed on the low counter of the receptionist's desk and then stepped to the higher part to get as elevated, and look as authoritative, as possible.

He spread his hands apart like Moses. He didn't waste time telling people to be calm, proclaim his authority, or try to reason with anyone. He simply yelled, "Hey! HEY!!! Y'ALL SHUT THE FUCK UUUUUPPPPP!!!" Holt found it funny, especially in their current surroundings, and decided that he was going to be friends with the man. The command had a limited effect on the people closest to him, but no sooner had he gotten their attention than the rest of the people swallowed them back up in panic. Holt jumped onto another counter and lent his own considerable voice to the effort. Between the two of them, they regained some order within the mob within a few minutes. Holt's throat felt shredded, but the job got done.

Mutt finally had everyone's attention. "Thank you. Listen up...I'm Sergeant Mutters. Some of you in here know me personally, by face, name, or stellar reputation. Doesn't matter, because if you're familiar with me at all, you know I'm not going to put up with this shit. Period. We will maintain order in here. Anybody has a problem with that, there's the window."

Mutt paused for a moment to see if there were any challenges. Holt wasn't exactly floored to see that there weren't any.

Mutt continued. "Okay, see that guy...wave, Holt...right over there? That's my new deputy, Holt. He's killed before, so I'd do what he says. He's going to be putting his team together, so if you are trained and can be trusted with a weapon, go see him. Now, who has medical training?" Several hands went up, and he motioned those people to him.

Well, I've just been voluntold, Holt thought. *That hasn't happened since I separated from the Air Force.* But someone had to do it.

He noticed that Anders was glaring at him, apparently upset that he'd been passed over for the spur of the moment promotion. He strode over to Holt, anyway. "Well, look at you, keeping my spot warm. What am I doing?"

Holt heard a familiar bell sound behind him, but it didn't register right away. "Find as many guys...or women, I don't care...with strong stomachs as you can. Then, we have to make nice with the head of building security, seeing as I stuck his own gun in his face. We'll need their help in locking this place d-"

Holt heard screams and whipped his head

145

around. It took him less than a second to realize what the bell sound had been.

The elevator.

From the garage.

No way, Holt had time to think before the doors opened. Chaos took over in just a few seconds. When he had a moment to reflect later, Holt thought that what had happened with the six passengers on the second floor elevator was even more horrifying than facing the thousands on the street. Holt immediately forgot about his problems and concentrated on the one thing he had the slightest control of: survival. He almost welcomed it.

When the doors opened, the unfortunates who were standing close were attacked immediately. A few, the lucky ones, died almost as quickly. The truth was that if everyone who was immediately attacked died they could have contained it right then and there; Holt, Mutt, and Anders were already moving with their weapons drawn and most likely could have dealt with the half dozen zombies before they did any more damage. As it happened, some died and the rest were turned with frightening speed. In some cases, only a few seconds passed between bite, death, and reanimation. There was no warning. Everyone else surged away as quickly as they could, but the bodies were already packed tightly and there was nowhere to retreat to. The slower, weaker ones were trampled underfoot.

The infection traveled outward like a ripple in a pond. Zombie infects human, human turns, new zombie infects another, rinse and repeat.

"The stairs!!!" Anders screamed, and Holt thought that was a great idea. He had no chance of

146

stemming the tide here, so he chose the better part of valor. Mutt apparently had the same idea, as did a few others. Those with weapons used them indiscriminately, as everything in their path either was a zombie or was turning into one. Anders made it first and slammed open the door. Holt had a vision of the man grinning crazily and slamming the door shut on everyone else, but he actually sent a few rounds in support, despite having already reached safety. Mutt, and several others caught up with him. Holt, the last one through, didn't bother taking another look before slamming the door and bracing it with his shoulder. He must have been spotted, because a vicious pounding commenced on the other side. A stocky black man added his bulk to Holt's, and Holt was grateful.

"We have anything to block this?!?" Holt bellowed.

One of the men who had made it was the security guard who Holt had drawn on earlier. If he held a grudge, he smartly didn't let it affect his current decision making. "The 3rd floor has a shitload of office furniture!"

"Go! Go! Everyone else help him! I don't give a fuck if you throw it down the stairs!"

Anders, Mutt, and the two others (Holt didn't notice that one was a woman until they came back) took the stairs two and three at a time and disappeared around a corner. A few seconds later they heard the 3rd floor door slamming shut.

The man next to him asked, "You think they're coming back?" He sounded out of breath. He looked in pretty good shape for his age (Holt guessed mid-50's), so Holt chalked it up to anxiety. He also knew there was a real chance that he sounded the same.

"Yeah. That cop is the real thing."

"Will it make a difference if they don't?"

Holt considered the circumstances, the magnitude of what they were facing. He didn't know how to honestly answer that question, so he said. "If they don't, the good news is I have enough bullets to kill us both several times."

"Oh, sorry, I didn't get you anything."

Holt chuckled. "Man with a sense of humor. I-"

The 3rd floor stairwell door slammed open again. "Coming down! Get ready to move your asses!" Mutt's duo back came into view. He and Anders were carrying a very heavy-looking wooden desk. When they got near the bottom they flipped it up the long way and got a good grip.

Holt's companion knew what they had in mind. "You good for three seconds?"

Holt dug in as hard as he could. "Go!"

He scrambled to his feet as the other men butted an edge of the desk up against the door. Holt was wedged, but he wriggled out and around it. Though the door was only unattended for two seconds, the lock almost buckled from the pounding. It held, barely, and the desk slammed into place. Holt and his partner resumed their positions, this time with a slab of wood between them and the door. The extra weight was a welcome addition, but Holt was a long way from comfortable. "Keep it coming!"

He didn't have to wait long. Right behind them was a similar desk. The woman who carried one end was slightly built, and she was obviously struggling, but she held her own. Dozens of pieces came down, and

Holt and his workmate Sam (Holt learned his name after the third desk) continued their dance until the furniture was packed tightly halfway up the stairwell. Then they relaxed, but not much.

"Come on," Mutt said. "Third floor's abandoned."

They all went upstairs. Abandoned was exactly the way to describe it. It was clear that the occupants of the offices had evacuated. It had the feel of a ghost town, which was a welcome respite from the pandemonium of the last few hours. They all collapsed in the chairs nearest to them. No one spoke for several moments. Holt thought that they might be in shock, but he just had nothing to say.

Anders broke the silence. "Damn, I dropped my smokes. Some zombie's probably lighting up on my dime right now."

The woman reached into her jacket pocket and produced a pack of clove cigarettes. "I've been trying to quit, so this is the best I can do."

"Works for me." He took two and walked over to the window. Holt wanted to think he was being polite, but the smart money said he was just antisocial.

She held the pack out to the group. "Anyone else?"

Sam took one. "What he said, except cigars."

Holt leaned over to Mutt. "This floor secured?"

"Yeah. We buried the other stairwell entrance, too. I don't think the elevator's going anywhere anymore."

"Nice." Holt picked up the phone handset on the desk closest to him. There was no dial tone. "Dead. But these phones might just be disconnected. There are a whole lot of other floors to check. Any vending machines?"

"I haven't seen any yet."

The woman said, "There's a break room down that hallway. The machines are in there. Water, too."

The rest of the group stared at her.

She peeked out from under her Red Sox cap. "I'm the senior network administrator here. Lena Moore."

"Okay. It's good to have someone who knows the lay of the land, so to speak. If you wouldn't mind, Lena, take..." He looked to the security guard. "...take Officer Salmon here and smash 'n grab those machines. It doesn't really matter what you take, just take a lot of it. After we catch our breath, I say we head up, floor by floor, until we find the ideal place to hole up and figure this thing out. Those barricades will probably hold, but I'm not betting my life on it. Holt?"

He thought on it, trying to find any flaws. "It's as good a plan as any."

"Got it. And call me Fish." He and Lena went about their task. She led him first to the supply closet where they grabbed trash bags, presumably to load them up with empty calories.

Holt had a thought. "Grab any batteries! And, sorry about the gun in your face thing!" The pair heard him. Fish held up a peace sign in acknowledgment as they split up, Lena to the supply room and Fish to the break area.

"Okay, do we even know what's above us?" Sam asked in between puffs of his cigarette. "It would make sense that the upper floors would be zombie...is that what we're calling them?...zombie-free. And that there are survivors, too. But the only way to know is to check each floor."

"Yup."

"Okay, then." He dropped his voice to a whisper. "Just don't pair me up with the guy at the window. He gives me the creeps."

"You and me both, Sam," Holt reassured him.

"Sarge! SARGE!" Fish's panicked voice sounded from the break room. Holt and Mutt drew at the same time, expecting to see a pack of zombies on the kid's tail, but he was waving a two-way radio instead. Lena was a few paces behind him. "I just got a transmission from downstairs! They got a radio off of another guard!"

"Say that again?"

"Hold on!" He put the two-way to his mouth and transmitted. "Last caller repeat!" He released the button and they all waited. Even Anders moved close enough to hear.

There was a crackle of static, then: "Thank God you're there! Me and a bunch of other people made it into the bathroom, but those things are trying to get in! Please help us!"

Five people kept passing looks to one another. All of their gazes settled on the sixth.

Holt grabbed the radio from Fish and held it out to Mutt. "You're the law," he said.

"What am I supposed to tell them? Congratulations on being alive, now smash a mirror and cut your own throats?"

Holt said nothing, but continued to offer the radio.

Mutt snatched it up with a grumbled curse. He

cleared his throat. "This is Sergeant Mutters of the LWPD. What's your name, caller?"

"It's Burt! Burt Allen!"

"Okay, Burt, how is everybody else?"

"Scared shitless!"

"That's understandable, of course." He released the mic and spoke to the group. "What am I supposed to do? I can't help them!"

"You know what to tell them, Mutters," Anders said. "You just told us."

Holt's watched the look of dawning horror come over his new friend's face. His heart broke for the Sergeant, and at that moment he decided he could be the bad guy. He took the radio from his shaking hands and walked away from the group. "Burt, my name is Cameron Holt." Pause. "Yeah, that guy."

Lena asked, "Wait, where's he going? What's he going to tell them?"

"He's going to tell them they should have moved faster, probably."

"You heartless asshole!" She pleaded with the others. "Isn't there anything...?"

"There's no hope for them, Lena," Fish said softly. "Zero."

The last thing they heard before Holt closed the door to the supply room was, "Do you have the guard's gun, too?"

Holt was gone for more than five minutes, but no one spoke. Anders wandered back over to the window and lit up his second cigarette, but no one else even sat down.

They heard a muffled gunshot. It sounded like it came from downstairs.

Maybe from a downstairs bathroom.

Another shot quickly followed the first, then another right on top of that. Silence again. They could hear Holt yelling, then screaming, from the supply room. Sam was closest, and he thought he could make out the words "do it" over and over again, getting louder each time.

There was one final shot, and silence. Holt didn't open the door for another five minutes. When he finally did, he didn't speak. He handed the radio back to Fish, slammed through the stairwell door, and headed up to the fourth floor.

Mutt felt ashamed that he let another man do the dirty work that, by virtue of his authority, should have been his. He owed that man a gigantic debt of honor, and he vowed to himself that he would spend the rest of his life, however long it might be, repaying it. In the meantime, he'd take control of the group again. Holt would need their support. "Okay, grab the food and drinks. Fish, is there another armory?"

The question seemed to take the younger man by surprise, but it snapped him out of his fugue. "What? Oh, uhhhh, no. Only in the main office, on the second floor. And I think we've established that that's a lost cause right now."

"Thought so. We'll figure it out on the way. Let's go."

They grabbed what they could and entered the stairwell more cautiously than Holt had a few moments before.

They searched each floor in turn, and were left with one question: where were all the patients?

"This makes dozens of people," Lena offered. "I

153

know some of them were...downstairs. I have no clue where the rest could have gone." She looked to Fish. "Did you guys run a fire drill?"

He shrugged his shoulders. "Not that I know of. Even if we did, I'd think that most people would have taken their coffees, at least." He cocked his head to his shoulder and stared. "That's weird."

"What?" Sam asked.

"Nothing. Just...thinking out loud."

"Maybe they went up?" Mutt said.

"That's an idea. What's on the upper floors, Lena?"

"The labs, executive offices, cafeteria. That's where I was headed; I was supposed to network a bunch of new machines in the labs when all of this kicked off."

"Up we go."

They climbed several more flights of stairs (peeking in to confirm the status of the next two floors) until they reached the 7th. Holt made to walk through it as he had all the others and nearly dislocated his shoulder. The door held firm. There were no locks, so it had to be barricaded from the inside. And to be barricaded from the inside, there would have to be people.

"Hey!" He pounded on the door. "Open up! We have survivors out here!" He got no answer. "Try the radio."

Fish started to cycle through the channels. "This is Security 2, anyone there? Hello?"

On channel 4, they got a response. "Security 2, this is Dr. Vincent. How many are you? Any wounded?"

"Six, and miraculously, no."

"Hang tight; we'll let you in."

* * *

Orpheus returned as Mutt finished up. "And that's how we met Martin Trager, head of hospital and kind of a prick. I don't like him, I sure as hell don't trust him, but we need him. And he needs what we can provide for him."

"Specimens?" Tim asked.

"Right. And our experience. We survived the initial outbreak with few weapons and no organization. Now we have some tools. It's not ideal, but it's mostly doable. Trager's a bureaucrat, not a grunt, like us. He never would have been able to put this together."

"He'd shit his pants if he ever had to fight one of those things," Sam said.

"And what do you get?"

"His resources."

"Resources to do what?"

Orpheus seemed surprised by the question. "Time to move out." He rose and the rest of the team followed, save for Tim, who remained seated.

"Hold on a sec. I volunteered to help you guys because I wanted to do something. I wanted to stop feeling useless. If I die doing it, so what. But if there's some other agenda here, your agenda..."

Orpheus stopped in his tracks and turned slowly, but not completely, toward Tim.

"I'd drop it if I were you, bait," Fish warned.

"...then I deserve to know what it is. I'm the only one who doesn't, and that's bullshit!"

Orpheus still hadn't faced Tim, but Mutt recognized his demeanor. It meant trouble. He kept quiet, but he got ready to peel Orpheus off of Tim.

"Sir, if you tell me what you're looking for, I can help you find it."

Orpheus said, "Stand up."

Tim did, and waited for whatever was coming. Orpheus put his hand inside his jumpsuit and Tim remembered what he'd been told about catching a bullet if Orpheus felt he couldn't trust him. He tried not to sweat.

Orpheus pulled out a small piece of paper.

A photo.

Tim took one look at it and knew.

"My son, Tim. I'm looking for my son."

It all came together for him then. The two teams, the walkies, the wedding ring, and the name. Orpheus. Tim had been right on the money. He tried to not stammer. "Thank you, sir. We'll find him."

Orpheus moved to the stairs, presumably to begin searching for valuables and collecting the walkies. Tim moved to follow him when another hand grabbed his wrist and stopped him.

Mutt said, "There's one other thing you need to know. There's almost no chance that his son's still alive. He's almost certainly one of them. And, in that case, no one puts him down but Orpheus...according to Orpheus, at least. But if that happens, there's no doubt in my mind that, no matter where we are or what we're doing, Orpheus will follow him about as quickly as it takes to pull the trigger once more. No one knows what happened to his wife, I have my theories, but the thought of finding his son alive or, worst case, putting him down for good, is the only thing keeping him going. So if you ever find the kid in the picture, the only person you don't tell is him. Got it?

"So you want me to disobey a direct order and deny a guy closure about his family?"

"He looks out for us; we look out for him. I don't care if you don't understand it."

"I understand just fine. I just want to make sure that the four of us right here are on the same page. For all I know, this is another one of your dumbass hazing things."

Sam, who had remained on the sidelines since they entered the building, said, "We don't pull that stuff down here. Ever."

"So what do I do if I find him?"

"Tell one of us. We'll figure it out. Chances are Orpheus will spot him long before we do, but we can try."

"This whole thing sucks."

"You know what sucks, bait?" Fish said. "I didn't hear that story for two damn weeks, teacher's pet."

"By the way, what did you see?" Tim asked.

"Huh?"

"When you first saw the evacuated floors."

"Oh, shit, I forgot about that. Well, check this: the whole...zombie...thing kicked off at what, six pm-ish on a Saturday, right?'

"Yeah. So?"

"So, we normally have a lot of people working Saturdays, that's not strange. What's odd is that I remember that the breakfast delivery came in at about 9:00 am. Coffee, donuts, bagels."

"I'm not following, Fish," Sam said.

"We've all worked in offices, and we know what happens when free food's involved. There's no way that breakfast stuff would last an hour, let alone all day. What I wondered then was, if that floor was evacuated, why was it evacuated like nine hours before there was anything to be evacuated from?"

* * *

They retrieved the walkies and whatever else useful they could find, then gathered around Orpheus and his city map. "Okay, this," He drew a large X over the building they were in. "...is clear. Retrieval is complete. Batteries in the walkies been swapped out?" He saw several nods. "Good. And I hope everyone's gone to the bathroom, because now we get in the shit again."

They secured the building as they left and backtracked to the intended reap zone. Orpheus didn't expect much in the way of a zombie presence. The "warehouse district" as it was called was a relative term. Mostly, it consisted of modest companies who had their operations and storage in the same place, such as the local window manufacturer and newspaper publisher. Those buildings would have been mostly if not completely evacuated right in the beginning, as they had a small number of employees with transportation easily accessible in their dedicated parking areas. Easy in, easy out.

Still, they were just as cautious as they would be anywhere else. Complacency killed. The sweeps didn't take long, and, as expected, they found no one, or thing, inside any of them. The large ventilation pipes and wide open spaces would make the burn even easier. The only thing that really stuck out in Orpheus' mind was in the printing room of the newspaper. The line of newspapers left abandoned on the press didn't proclaim "THE DEAD WALK THE EARTH" or other such nonsense like you saw in the movies. The headline had to do with island politics. Somehow, that was even more unsettling. The speed at which this thing had happened was frightening.

They dropped a smaller number of walkies than normal in and around those buildings and hoofed it to the theatre. They were acutely aware of the throng of zombies that still occupied the alley between the theatre and the library, drawn by their arrival, so they quietly slipped up the fire escape to the roof. The existence of the fire escape wasn't coincidence or a stroke of luck; it was another reason why they chose this insertion point.

Once on the roof, they took a breather, grabbed a quick snack, and checked their gear. Sam grabbed several pairs of handcuffs and a pole with a loop on the end of it, similar to what a dog catcher would use to corral a rabid dog.

Tim had an uneasy feeling what those meant.

They made the leap back to the library roof and gathered around the door. Mutt asked him what the plan was. Orpheus said, "I'm almost positive that there's a Jekyll somewhere on the other side of that door. Unfortunately, I have no idea what else might be. So, my big plan is to open this door and wing it."

Tim surprised himself when he said, "I'll do it."

His comment was met with four furrowed brows.

"Not likely," Mutt snapped. "You can be the first one to cover me, though. How's that?"

"Come on, Orpheus! You had no problem setting me loose in the theater. I could have just as easily been killed there. Let me take the lead. I'm ready."

"You're not ready for a Jekyll; no one ever is. Maybe someday." Believing he had made his point, he took Mutt's weapon and replaced it with one of the poles. "Slip this over its head and don't let go. Don't hesitate. And for Christ's sake, don't trust it. Just loop it and move back to the stairs as quickly as you can."

"Got it."

Orpheus put his hand on the knob. "Sam, Fish, when we get to a safe place you two are on cuffs."

"Hey, thanks," Fish said.

Orpheus looked to Tim. "Don't engage unless I do."

Tim nodded.

"Wait for my signal. Do nothing until I say." Orpheus cracked the door open and Mutt pushed his light in a few inches. He swept it left to right and back again. He stopped on a hunched shape near the base of the stairs. Its back was to them, and it appeared to be alone. It was moving, swaying, back and forth in one spot. Orpheus appreciated the small favor. He said, "That's your target. Grab and go." He swung the door open wide enough to accommodate all of them.

Tim moved fast. He yanked the pole out of Mutt's unsuspecting hand and pushed past Orpheus into the stairwell.

Orpheus growled, "Get your fuckin' ass back here!"

Tim shook his head vehemently and put several stairs in between them. He was committed now.

"Godammit, cover him," Orpheus said to his

team.

Tim gulped. He moved very slowly, making absolutely sure of each step before he made the next. All he could see in his mind was him falling down the steps and getting savaged while everyone else was already thinking about his replacement. He was pretty sure he was being unfair to them, but he couldn't help but think that three guys previously in his position had probably been less paranoid, and now they were dead.

Tim got to the last step and he thought he heard something coming from the thing's direction. He strained to hear it and thought that it might be mumbling something. *Don't trust it*, Orpehus had insisted. So Tim didn't. He moved close enough to loop the apparatus around its neck. He looked to either side of him instinctively; nothing else appeared in the dull red glow. He held his breath and extended.

Just like playing "Operation" when I was a kid.

He had about a foot left to go when he heard it say, "Not fair." It said it over and over. He reflexively said, "Sir?" and kicked himself for it. The thing whirled around.

It looked human. And then it screamed, a monster unleashed.

Tim knew that he'd made a huge mistake. He slammed the loop downward and was lucky enough to get it around the neck. The thing lunged at him. The pole was strong, and Tim had a firm grip, but the forward momentum knocked him onto his back. It kept screaming.

Each floor of the library was a great circle around a central atrium. There were two wide staircases at each end. Tim felt more than heard a change in his

161

situation. The Jekyll hadn't been alone, after all. He was just separated from the rest of the zombies in the library, and they were all coming now. Most slowly, but too many swiftly.

The Jekyll was still screaming and trying to get at Tim. Because of the pole, it couldn't reach him; its flailing arms passed a foot from Tim's face. Due to its weight, however, Tim couldn't get to his feet, either. The end of the pole was braced against the floor and steadied under Tim's armpit; it probably wouldn't seem like it to an observer, but Tim had control. He just couldn't risk moving. He'd screwed up the approach for sure, but he was going to follow Orpheus' other order to hold on if it killed him and trust that they would save his ass again.

There was no pretense of stealth anymore, so the rest of the team turned on their high-powered lights and waded into combat. Some Sprinters were on top of them in the blink of an eye. Several well-placed rounds knocked them backwards and sideways, but they were moving too fast to get an easy headshot. The team couldn't concentrate solely on them either, because though the slower ones moved at a walking pace, they hadn't had much ground to cover. Everywhere Tim looked he saw pairs of legs closing in on him. He started to slide towards the roof stairs by doing a sort of wriggle on his butt and shoulders, still scraping the pole along the ground. It was slow going, but each inch further away from the zombies was worth it.

He was almost to the stairs when a zombie fell down, its kneecaps blown off, right next to him. Its jaws were only a few feet away from Tim's face, and he had no time to think. He hoped he could hold the pole with one hand for a second or two, pulled his sidearm, and blew a hole in its face.

Lacking the other arm to steady the pole, the Jekyll managed to twist sideways and yank the pole out of Tim's hand. It thrashed the pole to the side and dove for Tim again, this time with nothing in its path.

The thing was stopped in mid-dive by Orpheus, who had managed to secure the pole. He wrestled it towards the stairs and yelled, "Let's go! Let's go!" Tim scrambled to his feet and added his firepower to keep the zombies at bay. Orpheus had already dragged the Jekyll through the door and onto the roof. The rest of them were only a few seconds behind. Mutt, who brought up the rear, slammed the door. Mutt and Tim leaned against the door, the other three subdued the Jekyll. Sam and Fish cuffed its wrists, ankles, and they threw a thick canvas bag over its head and secured it with a drawstring.

Orpheus informed Lena that they had a Jekyll in tow and called for an extraction. They had about ten minutes to wait.

Tim wasn't quite caught off-guard by the rough hands that slammed him against the door. What was unexpected was the impact itself; it drove the air out of him.

"What the fuck was that?!?" Orpheus screamed. "What did I say? I told you to sit this one out. Seeing as you were too stupid to understand that part, I at least hoped you would have followed instructions. Grab and hustle the fuck out of there! It's not hard! Listen to me next time, Eth-!" He paused, took an extended breath, and said, "You're the first person who didn't do what I told them who is actually around to have a next time, you lucky little shit."

"Yes, sir," was all Tim could manage to force out.

The Jekyll settled down after a few minutes. It began mumbling again.

When Tim felt it was safe to speak again, he asked, "What is that thing, anyway? I thought it was a survivor. I...froze."

Orpheus nodded in agreement and could have beaten him up further over it, but he didn't. "The Jekylls are somewhere between us and them. They slip back and forth from mindless zombie to nearly-human lucidity. That's why they're so damn dangerous."

"But we got him!" Fish whooped and high-fived Sam. "Let's go get another one!"

"Pass," Mutt said. "I just want to relax."

"I bet you do," Fish said. "Maybe O will put in a good word for you."

"Aw, shut up."

"Knock it off. Grab our gear and prepare for extraction." Orpheus grabbed a walkie and transmitted, "Attention, any survivors. Please respond immediately." He waited for a few moments and got nothing. "Ethan Holt." He paused. "Ethan, are you there?" He was disappointed, as he had been for weeks, but not surprised. He repeated the transmission several more times, then replaced the radio on his belt.

Mutt patted him on the shoulder. "Next time, buddy."

By the time the helicopter arrived they all had their bags slung on their backs. The pilot hovered and the co-pilot threw down a rope ladder and a body harness. Orpheus and Tim stayed on the roof and strapped the Jekyll into the harness while the others ascended. Orpheus gave a thumbs-up and they reeled the Jekyll in. When it was completely in the helicopter and secured, Mutt signaled for the other two to join them.

Tim went first, and as he slung his leg over the top rung and onto the floor of the helicopter, Orpheus began to climb. A few rungs from the top he stopped and looked down at the dead island in the predawn light. It was another miss, and he was running out of opportunities.

ORPHEUS – JULY2011

About the author:

Dan DeWitt lives with his wife and son in Upstate New York. He has been writing fiction for what seems like forever, and he's picked up at least a few useful tips that he likes to share from time to time at http://dandewittfiction.blogspot.com/. He has published a handful of short stories online; all but one of the ezines are defunct, and he's trying to not take that personally. Underneath is his first short story collection. In July, his full-length zombie thriller Orpheus will hit the shelves. After that, he hopes to be much, much busier.

18211684R00088

Made in the USA
Lexington, KY
21 October 2012